VERMILLION

W9-ACD-082

DISCARDED
BY THE
VERMILLION PUBLIC
LIBRARY

Maigret
at the
Coroner's

Originally published in

England under the title

Maigret and the Coroner

**Georges
Simenon**

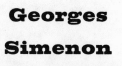

MAIGRET
AT THE
CORONER'S

Translated by Frances Keene

A Helen and Kurt Wolff Book

Harcourt Brace Jovanovich

New York and London

© 1952 by Georges Simenon
English translation copyright © 1980 by Georges Simenon

All rights reserved. No part of
this publication may be reproduced or
transmitted in any form or by any means,
electronic or mechanical, including photocopy,
recording, or any information storage and
retrieval system, without permission
in writing from the publisher.

Library of Congress Cataloging in Publication Data

Simenon, Georges, 1903–
Maigret at the coroner's.

Translation of Maigret chez le coroner.
"A Helen and Kurt Wolff book."
I.   Title.
PZ4.S5848Mai   [PQ2637.I53]   843′.912   80–81491
ISBN 0–15–155556–7

Printed in the United States of America

First American edition

B C D E

This translation is dedicated

to the memory of

Stefan Congrat-Butlar.

FRANCES KEENE

DISCARDED
BY THE
VERMILLION PUBLIC
VERMILLIONRY
PUBLIC LIBRARY
VERMILLION, S. D.

47097

Maigret
at the
Coroner's

1

Maigret,
Deputy Sheriff

"Hey, you!"

Maigret turned around, as if he had been in school, to see who was being called on.

"Yes, you, over there . . ."

And the lean old man with the huge white mustache who seemed a living evocation of the Old Testament held out a trembling arm. But toward whom? Maigret looked at the man beside him, then at the woman on the other side. Finally, embarrassed, he saw that everyone had turned to look at him, including the coroner, the Air Force sergeant who was on the stand, the district attorney, the jurors, and even the sheriffs.

"Who, me?" he asked, half rising and very much surprised that they should need to call on him.

All the faces looking his way were smiling, as if everyone were in on some joke save himself.

"Yes, you," said the old man who looked like Ezekiel but whose mustache also made Maigret think of Clemenceau. "Hurry up and put out that pipe!"

He could not even remember having lit it. Rattled, he

sat down once more, muttering excuses. His neighbors were laughing by now, but it was a friendly laugh.

It was not a dream. He was wide awake. It was he, Chief Superintendent of Detectives Maigret, of the Paris police force, who was there—more than six thousand miles from home—sitting in the audience at a coroner's inquest. It was he, Maigret, looking as serious and well-brought-up as a bank clerk, despite the fact that he was wearing neither coat nor vest.

He was perfectly aware that his colleague Cole had courteously "shelved" him, but he could not hold it against him since he would have done exactly as the FBI officer had were their positions reversed. Had he not acted exactly the same when, two years earlier, he had been assigned to pilot his colleague Pyke, of Scotland Yard, on his visit to France? And hadn't he often left Pyke at some terrace café, just like a checked umbrella, flashing him a reassuring smile: "I'll be back in a moment"?

There was the difference that the Americans were more friendly. Whether in New York or in one of the ten or eleven states he had been through since, people would tap him on the shoulder: "What's your first name?"

He couldn't very well tell them he didn't have one. The result was that he had to admit he was called Jules. His interlocutors would pause to consider a moment. Then, "Oh, *yes* . . . Julius!"

Julius, pronounced in the American manner, already seemed to him a little less distressing than Jules.

"Have a drink, Julius!"

Thus it happened that, in an incalculable number of bars, he had drunk an incalculable number of bottles of beer, Manhattan cocktails, and shots of whiskey.

He'd already had drinks a while ago, before lunch, with

the Mayor of Tucson and the county sheriff, to whom Harry Cole had introduced him.

What amazed him the most was not the surroundings, not the people, but the fact that he, Maigret, was here in a city in Arizona and that, for example, he was seated as now on a bench in a little courtroom presided over by a justice of the peace.

They had had drinks before lunch, but that foretold nothing. With the meal, they had been served ice water. The mayor had been very nice. As for the sheriff, he had awarded him some sort of piece of paper with a handsome plaque in silver to back it up. Just as happens in cowboy films, Maigret had been made a deputy sheriff.

It was the ninth or tenth such award he had received. He had been made a deputy sheriff in eight or nine counties of New Jersey, Maryland, Virginia, North or South Carolina—he was no longer sure which—and Texas, not to mention the city of New Orleans.

In Paris, he had often played host to foreign colleagues but this was the first time he had made a similar junket, a study tour, it was called officially, "to get acquainted with American methods."

"You should spend a few days in Arizona before you get to California. It's on your way."

Everything was always on his way. Following this formula, he had covered hundreds of miles. What the Americans called "a bit out of your way" was a detour of three or four days.

"It's right nearby!"

This meant that it was once or twice the distance from Paris to Marseilles, and that he could travel a whole day in the Pullman car without seeing a real city.

"Tomorrow," the FBI man, Cole, had told him, "we'll go

take a look at the Mexican–American frontier. It's right nearby!" It was Cole who had him in tow in Arizona.

This time, the goal was only some fifty or sixty miles away.

"You'll find it interesting. The place is called Nogales, a frontier town half in one country, half in the other. That's where most of the marijuana comes over the border."

Maigret had learned that the Mexican-grown plant had more or less replaced the appeal of the higher-priced drugs, opium and cocaine.

"That's the spot where most of the cars stolen in California cross over the border, too."

Meanwhile, Harry Cole had shelved him. He must have had something to do this afternoon.

"It just happens that a coroner's inquest is being aired this afternoon. Would you like to see how we run one?"

He had brought Maigret to the courthouse, seated him on one of the three benches of the little room with its white walls and its American flag in a stand behind the judge's chair, and explained to Maigret that the justice of the peace would be acting as coroner. Cole had not told him that he would be leaving him completely on his own. Then the FBI man had gone to shake a few hands, clap a few people on the shoulder, and had told Maigret, casually: "I'll come by to pick you up later."

The French detective did not know what case was being heard. No one in the room was wearing a jacket. True, the temperature outside was over 110 degrees. The six jurors were seated on the same bench as himself, at the other end, near the door. The group included one Negro, one Indian with a strong jaw, a Mexican who looked a little like a cross between the other two, and a rather elderly woman who wore a flower-printed dress and a strange little hat planted well forward on her head.

6

Every so often, Ezekiel would get up and try to regulate the enormous fan turning lazily at ceiling height, which was making so much noise that it was hard to hear what was going on.

Things seemed to be going well enough. In France, Maigret would have said that the case was being handled "family style." The coroner sat on a kind of podium, wearing an immaculate white shirt and a flowered silk tie.

The witness, or the accused, Maigret was not quite sure which, was seated in a chair not far from him. He was an Air Force sergeant in a beige dress uniform. There were four more of them, all seated in a line facing the jury and looking like overgrown schoolboys.

"Tell us what happened on the night of July 27."

This young man turned out to be Sergeant Ward, a name Maigret had heard. He was at least six feet tall and had blue eyes under heavy black brows that met above the bridge of his nose.

"I went to get Bessie at her house around seven-thirty."

"Speak louder. Turn toward the jury. Can you hear him, jurors?"

They indicated that they could not hear, and Sergeant Ward cleared his throat so he could speak up more strongly.

"I went to get Bessie at her house around seven-thirty."

Maigret had to make a double effort to understand because he had had no opportunity to practice spoken English since he had been in high school. Words escaped him and turns of phrase eluded him.

"You are married and have two children, Sergeant?"

"Yes, sir."

"How long have you known Bessie Mitchell?"

The sergeant thought, like a good pupil before answering a teacher's question. For an instant, he flicked a glance

7

at someone seated beside Maigret whose identity the Paris detective had not yet ascertained.

"About six weeks."

"Where did you meet her?"

"In a drive-in where she was a waitress."

Maigret had been introduced to drive-ins. Often the members of the force who had been detailed to pilot him around had drawn up at a drive-in, especially toward evening, bringing their cars to a halt before one of those small roadside restaurants. No one would get out of the car. A young woman would approach to take their orders, and would bring them sandwiches, hot dogs, or spaghetti, on a platter tray that attached to the car door.

"Did you have sexual relations with her?"

"Yes, sir."

"The first evening you met?"

"Yes, sir."

"Where did this take place?"

"In the car. We parked in the desert."

The desert, all sand and cactuses, began at the very outskirts of the town. There were even patches of desert between certain areas of the city itself.

"Did you see her often after the time you first met?"

"About three times a week."

"And you would have relations with her each time?"

"No, sir."

Maigret almost expected to hear the little nit-picking judge ask, "Why not?"

Instead, his question was, "How many times?"

"Once a week, sir."

Maigret saw not a flicker of a smile on anyone's face except the commissioner's.

"Always in the desert?"

"In the desert or at her house."

8

"Did she live alone?"

Sergeant Ward's eyes sought a face up and down the assembled spectators. Finally, he pointed out a young woman seated to Maigret's left.

"She lived with Erna Bolton."

"What did you do on July 27 after you had called for Bessie Mitchell at her house?"

"I took her to the Penguin Bar where my friends were waiting for me."

"What friends?"

This time Ward pointed to the four other Air Force men and named them as he indicated each one.

"Dan Mullins, Jimmy Van Fleet, O'Neil, and Wo Lee."

The last named was a Chinese who looked barely sixteen.

"Were there any other people with you at the Penguin?"

"Not at our table."

"Were there people at other tables?"

"Bessie's brother, Harold Mitchell, was there." As he pointed him out, Maigret realized Mitchell was his right-hand neighbor, the young man he had noticed because he had a painful-looking boil under his left ear.

"Was he alone?"

"No. He was with Erna Bolton, the musician, and Maggie."

"How old was Bessie Mitchell?"

"She told me she was twenty-three."

"Did you know that she was really only seventeen and that, being underage, she had no legal right to drink in a bar?"

"No, sir."

"Are you sure her brother had not told you how old she was?"

"He told me later, when we'd gone to the musician's.

That's when she'd started drinking whiskey from the bottle. He told me he didn't want her drinking, and he didn't want people to give her anything to drink. He said she was a minor and that he was responsible for keeping an eye on her."

"Did you also not know that Bessie had been married and divorced?"

"No. I knew that, sir."

"Had you promised to marry her?"

Sergeant Ward hesitated visibly.

"Yes, sir."

"Did you want to get a divorce to marry her?"

"I told her I would do it."

In the doorway stood a big deputy sheriff—a colleague! —in yellowish linen pants and an open-necked shirt. At his waist he wore a huge leather belt studded with cartridges, and an enormous horn-handled revolver hung against his thigh.

"Did you all have something to drink together?"

"Yes, sir."

"Did you have a lot to drink? About how many drinks apiece?"

"Each of us?" Ward shut his eyes for a moment to do a quick mental calculation. "I didn't count but, given the number of rounds, I'd say we had between fifteen and twenty beers."

"Apiece?"

Ward answered very candidly, "Yes, sir, not counting a few whiskeys."

It seemed curious to Maigret that no one appeared particularly surprised.

"Wasn't it at the Penguin that you had an argument with Bessie's brother?"

"Yes, sir."

"Did he reproach you for having relations with his sister, you being a married man?"

"No, sir."

"What was the reason you argued, then?"

"Because I'd asked him to give me back some money he owed me."

"Did he owe you much?"

"About five dollars."

Scarcely enough to pay one of those famous rounds at the Penguin Bar.

"Did you come to blows?"

"No, sir. We went out on the sidewalk. That's where we cleared things up between us. And we came back in to have a drink together."

"Were you drunk by then?"

"Not so's to notice it, sir."

"Did anything else happen at the Penguin?"

"No, sir."

"In short, you'd all been drinking. You drank until one in the morning, the time when the bar closes up, right?"

"Yes, sir."

"Was one of your pals making a play for Bessie?"

Sergeant Ward paused a moment before admitting: "Sergeant Mullins."

"Did you speak to him about it?"

"No. I just fixed it so he wouldn't sit beside her."

His friend Mullins was of the same height as he, also dark-haired, the type of man the girls must have thought a "knock-out." He vaguely reminded Maigret of a film star but he couldn't recall exactly which.

"Well, what happened at one o'clock when the bar closed?"

"We went over to the musician's place, Tony Lacour."

This man, too, must have been in the courtroom, but Maigret did not know which he was.

"Who paid for the two bottles of whiskey you took out with you?"

"I think Wo Lee paid for one of them."

"Did he drink with you, then, during the evening?"

"No, sir. Corporal Wo Lee does not drink or smoke. But he insisted on paying for something."

"How large is the musician's apartment?"

"A bedroom . . . a little living room . . . a bathroom, and a kitchen. . . ."

"How did you all fit into that apartment? What rooms were you in?"

"In all of them, sir."

"In what room did you quarrel with Bessie?"

"In the kitchen. I found Bessie drinking whiskey out of the bottle. That wasn't the first time, either."

"You mean the first time that evening?"

"I mean she had done it often, before the night of July 27. I didn't want her to drink too much, because afterwards she was sick."

"Was Bessie alone in the kitchen?"

"She was with him," and he indicated Mullins with a tilt of his chin.

It was at this point that Maigret, who had felt sleepy and heavy just a short time before, Maigret, who knew nothing of the case, found himself opening his mouth as if he were on the point of uttering a question that burned his lips.

The attorney asked, "Who suggested going to spend the rest of the night at Nogales?"

"It was Bessie."

"What time could it have been then?"

12

"About three in the morning. Maybe two-thirty."

Nogales was the frontier town Harry Cole had wanted to take Maigret to visit. In Tucson the bars closed at one, but on the other side of the frontier everything was open all night long.

"Who got into your car?"

"Bessie and my four friends."

"Didn't Bessie's brother go with you? What about Erna Bolton, or the musician and Maggie Wallach?"

"No, sir."

"Do you know what they went on to do?"

"No, sir."

"How were you seated in the car at the start?"

"Bessie was in front, seated between me and Sergeant Mullins. The three others were in the rear."

"Didn't you stop the car a little outside Tucson?"

"Yes, sir."

"At that point, you asked Bessie to change places. Why?"

"So that she wouldn't still be seated next to Dan Mullins."

"You put her in the back and Corporal Van Fleet came to take her place in front. Didn't you care that she was behind your back in the dark with the two others?"

Suddenly, without any foreseeable justification, the coroner barked, "Adjourned!"

He got up and made his way to the neighboring office on the glass door of which the word PRIVATE had been painted. Ezekiel pulled an enormous pipe from his pocket and, as he started to light it, he cast an odd look at Maigret.

Everybody went out, the jurors, the Air Force men, the women, the few curious onlookers.

They were on the ground floor of a big building con-

13

structed in Spanish style around a patio flanked by colonnades. One wing housed the jail, and the other the various administrative services of the county.

The five Air Force fellows had gone to sit on the balustrade that bordered the colonnade, and Maigret noted that not one of them spoke a word to any of the others. It was extremely hot. In one corner there was a red vending machine from which people retrieved a bottle of Coca-Cola after having inserted a coin.

Nearly everyone converged there, including a gentleman with gray hair who appeared to be the county district attorney. And they all drank from the bottle directly, placing the empty in a bin located alongside.

Maigret felt a little like a boy at his first recess in a new school. Still, he no longer wanted Harry Cole to pick him up right away.

He had never appeared in a courtroom before without a jacket, and this question of clothing had posed certain problems. As soon as he had crossed the state line into Virginia, he had realized that he could no longer spend his days in a three-piece suit and starched collar. Furthermore, all his life he had worn suspenders. His trousers, tailored in France, rose halfway up his chest.

He no longer remembered in which city one of his colleagues had taken him into a local department store— "No two ways about it . . ."—and made him buy a pair of lightweight pants like the ones he saw on all the men hereabouts. In addition, he had bought a wide leather belt on whose silver-colored buckle a bull's head was incised.

Others, coming in from the east, were less inhibited than he and rushed to outfit themselves in cowboy fashion from head to foot.

14

He noticed that the jurors, average-looking people who seemed easygoing enough, still wore high-heeled boots under their pants, and that some of them had multi-colored designs on their boots.

The short-handled revolvers that the sheriffs sported at their belts fascinated him because they were exactly like those he had seen, since childhood, in the Western films.

"Come on, jurors!" Ezekiel summoned them informally like a schoolmaster gathering his flock.

He clapped his hands, emptied his pipe and obliquely eyed Maigret's.

Maigret no longer felt so unfamiliar with the scene. He found his place, with the single difference that Harold Mitchell, Bessie's brother with the boil, was now seated next to Erna Bolton and they were talking in subdued tones. Maigret realized that it was he who had separated them.

He could not yet be sure that, in this account of beers, whiskeys, and once-a-week sexual encounters, there was a corpse. What he did know, because he had witnessed something similar in England, was the prescribed course of a coroner's inquest.

In proper fashion, almost meekly, Ward had returned to his place in the witness box. Ezekiel was once more wrestling with the big fan, and the coroner resumed nonchalantly:

"You stopped the car about eight miles from the city, a little beyond the municipal airfield. Why?"

Maigret had not grasped the total import and felt lucky that Ward once more was speaking so low he was asked to repeat his answer. The big fellow's blushes helped Maigret to understand his reply.

"Latrine duty, sir."

15

Perhaps he could not think of any other phrase decent enough for a court hearing with which to say that they all needed to pee.

"Did everyone get out of the car?"

"Yes, sir. I went some thirty feet away."

"Alone?"

"No, sir. With him!"

And he indicated Mullins, against whom he seemed to have a grudge.

"Do you know where Bessie went at that time?"

"I suppose she wandered off, too."

It was hard not to evoke the twenty-odd beers each of them had ingested.

"What time could it have been by then?"

"I suppose between three and three-thirty in the morning. I'm not sure, exactly."

"Did you see Bessie when you turned back to the car?"

"No, sir."

"What about Mullins?"

"He got back a few moments later."

"Where from?"

"I don't know."

"What did you say to your friends?"

"I said, 'To hell with that girl! That'll teach her a good lesson!' "

"Why?"

"Because she'd pulled the same trick on me before."

"What trick had she pulled?"

"Going off, dropping me, without saying where she was going."

"That's when you made a U-turn?"

"Yes. I drove a hundred yards or so toward Tucson and then I stopped and got out."

"Why?"

"I figured that she'd try to join us in the car, and I wanted to give her the chance to."

"Was she drunk?"

"Yes, sir. But she'd pulled that before, too. She still knew what she was doing."

"Where did you go when you got out of the car?"

"I walked toward the railroad tracks that parallel the highway about fifty yards farther out in the desert."

"Did you go as far as the embankment?"

"Yes, sir. I must have covered over a hundred yards of roadbed. I stopped at just about the spot where Bessie left us. I was calling her name."

"Loudly?"

"Yes, but I didn't see her. She didn't answer. I figured she just wanted to make me mad."

"Then you went back to your car. Didn't your friends say anything when you started the car and headed back for Tucson without troubling about Bessie any more?"

"No, sir."

"Do you consider you acted like a gentleman by leaving a woman in the desert in the middle of the night?"

Ward did not answer. He had lowered his head and Maigret, looking at the forehead with its heavy brows, began to sense something pigheaded and brutish about him.

"Did you go directly back to your base?"

The base, Davis Monthan, was one of the central rallying points for B-29s. It was located some six miles from Tucson in a different direction from Nogales.

"No, sir. I left three of my friends in town, near the bus depot."

"You kept one of them with you. Which one?"

"Sergeant Mullins."

"Why?"

17

"I wanted to go back and look for Bessie."

"So you turned around again and took the road back toward Nogales?"

"Yes, sir. I stopped at about the same spot I'd stopped the first time."

"Did you go back to the railroad tracks?"

There was a fairly long silence.

"No. I don't think so. I don't remember having got out of the car."

"What did you do?"

"I don't know. I woke up at the wheel with the car headed back to Tucson and a telegraph pole right in front of me. I remember the telegraph pole and a cactus nearby."

"Was Mullins still with you?"

"He was asleep beside me, his chin on his chest."

"In short, you have no recollection of what went on before you awoke in front of the telegraph pole?"

From the way Ward's lips trembled, Maigret understood that he was about to say something significant.

"No, sir. I had been drugged."

"You mean to tell me you were not drunk?"

"I've often had that much to drink and more. I've never passed out. No one has ever been able to drink me under the table. I know my own capacity. That night, I had been drugged."

"Could someone had slipped something in your glass earlier?"

"Or in a cigarette. When I woke up, I reached automatically for a cigarette from the pack in my pocket. I found a Camel; usually I smoke only Chesterfields. I smoked the Camel and then I passed out again."

"Still with Mullins beside you?"

"Yes."

18

"Do you suspect that Mullins slipped some doped cigarettes into the pack in your pocket?"

"Perhaps."

"Did you mention this to him when you woke up?"

"No."

"Didn't you speak to him?"

"No. I drove the car back to my place. I live in town with my wife and children. Mullins came up to the apartment. I tossed a pillow at him so's he could catch some sleep on the couch. I went to sleep."

"For how long?"

"I don't know. Maybe an hour. At six o'clock I went to the base to check out my jobs. I put my plane, the one assigned to my care, in flying condition."

"Exactly what does your job consist of?"

"I'm a mechanic. I verify the condition of the plane before take-off and I stay on the field."

"What did you do then?"

"I left the base around eleven in the morning."

"Alone?"

"With Dan Mullins."

"When did you learn of Bessie's death?"

"At about three in the afternoon."

"Where were you?"

"In a bar on Fifth Avenue. Mullins and I were having a beer."

"Had you had a lot to drink since you'd left the base?"

"Maybe ten or twelve bottles of beer. A sheriff came in and asked me if I was Sergeant Ward. I told him I was, and he asked me to follow him."

"You didn't yet know Bessie Mitchell was dead?"

"No, sir."

"And you didn't know that your other three friends had taken a taxi right after you'd left them at the bus depot

19

and had gone back over the same road toward Nogales?"

"No, sir."

"You didn't see any taxi on the road? You neither saw nor heard a train coming from Nogales?"

"No, sir."

"At the base that morning did you run into any one of your other three friends?"

"I ran across O'Neil."

"Didn't he tell you anything?"

"I don't exactly remember how he put it, but he said something like, 'As far as Bessie's concerned, everything's O.K.'"

"What did you make out of that?"

"That she'd probably made it home by hitching rides."

"You didn't go to her house to find out?"

"Yes. When we left the base at eleven that morning, we went by the house and Erna told me that Bessie hadn't been home all night."

"This was after Sergeant O'Neil had told you everything was O.K.?"

"Yes."

"Didn't this seem contradictory to you?"

"I just figured she'd gone somewhere else."

"You told us a while ago that you intended to get a divorce in order to marry Bessie."

"Yes, sir."

"Do you swear that you never saw Bessie again after she had gone away from the car with Sergeant Mullins?"

"Not living, no."

"Did you see her dead?"

"At the morgue, when the sheriff took me there."

"Sergeant Mullins was not in the car when you got back in behind the wheel after your first stop, and he only came back a few moments later?"

"That's right, sir."

"Any questions, Mr. Attorney?"

The lawyer with the graying hair shook his head.

Same negative indications from the five men and one woman jury members. The latter, in anticipation of the coroner's words, was already getting out her knitting.

"Session adjourned!"

Ezekiel lit his pipe. Maigret did the same. Everyone rushed as before into the corridor and looked for a coin in his or her pocket to feed into the red Coca-Cola machine.

Some people, however, entered a mysterious door. Maigret guessed they were more in-the-know than the rest of them, himself included, for when they came out their breaths smelled of alcohol.

At bottom, he was not too sure of the reality of everything taking place around him. The old black juror with close-cropped hair, wearing steel-rimmed glasses, looked at him smiling, as if they were already pals, and Maigret smiled back.

VERMILLION
PUBLIC LIBRARY
VERMILLION, S. D.

47097

2

The Top Boy
in Class

Once in a while one sees in a neighborhood café, particularly in a small town, someone who has wandered in because he is lost, or because he must wait for a train or a meeting. Seated on a bench, bored and half asleep, he vaguely follows a card game being played out at a nearby table.

Clearly he does not know the game, but soon his interest is caught and he would like to understand. Little by little, he leans forward to catch a glimpse of the cards in the partners' hands. According to how they play, he gives unconscious signs of approbation or distress, and the moment comes when he is hard put not to interrupt.

Maigret now saw himself acting a bit like the outsider in the provincial café and he was embarrassed. But he had no choice. He had been bitten: he wanted to know the outcome of the game.

During the questioning of Sergeant Ward, he had caught himself stirring impatiently on his bench. There were questions that the merest neophyte on his staff would not have failed to ask and that the little judge, so meticulous in his dress and gestures, seemed not to have thought of.

Of course, the coroner's inquest was not the trial. What these jurors had to decide was whether, according to them, Bessie Mitchell had died of natural causes, whether her death was accidental, or whether it was due to malevolence or a criminal act.

As for the rest, in either of the two final hypotheses the trial would be heard before another jury.

"Tell us what took place on July 27 after seven-thirty in the evening."

Wasn't it a little simple-minded to let the four young Air Force men listen to the testimony of their friend?

Sergeant O'Neil was shorter, more stocky than the others. His light hair had a reddish tinge to it and was wavy. With his heavy features, he reminded Maigret of a peasant from the north of France, albeit a scrubbed and slicked-up one.

Scrubbed they all were, everyone in the room. These people had a look of general good health and cleanliness that is rarely seen in an equivalent European crowd.

"We went to the Penguin and had a few drinks."

This one was the good boy of the class, not necessarily the intelligent student but the fellow who kept at it. Before answering, he would raise his eyes to the ceiling, again as if at school, taking time to think, then speaking slowly, in a flat, neutral tone of voice, turning toward the jurors as he had been asked to do.

In short, they were schoolboys, overgrown schoolboys twenty or more years old, solidly built, muscular, but boys nonetheless whom one might have mistaken for grownups.

"How many beers did you drink?"

"About twenty."

"Who paid for the rounds of drinks?"

This one remembered. After a pause—because he took his time before answering each question—he announced that Ward had paid for two rounds and that Dan Mullins had paid for almost all the rest. He himself had paid for one round only.

Maigret would have liked a face-to-face interview with this fellow in his office on the Quai des Orfèvres. He would have treated him to a thorough overhauling, just to see what sort of stuff he was made of.

One of the questions he would have asked him, among others, was, "Have you a mistress?" All except Ward were bachelors.

This ruddy-cheeked boy must have strong sexual appetites, and on the evening in question there were five fellows with a single girl. Besides, all of them except the young Chinese were passably drunk. Had not hands strayed in the rear seat in the dark of the car?

The coroner, it seemed, did not think along these lines or, if he did, he made no reference to the subject.

"Who was it decided to wind up the night in Nogales?"

"I don't remember exactly. I thought it was Ward."

"Did you hear Bessie suggest it?"

"No, sir."

"How were you seated in the car?"

One would have said that he had not been listening to his friend's testimony, it took him so long to reply.

"After a few moments, he made Bessie get into the back seat."

"Why?"

"Jealous of Mullins, I guess."

"Had he any more reason to be jealous of Mullins than of the rest of you?"

24

"I don't know."

"What happened once the car had passed the airport?"

"We stopped."

"For what reason?"

He took even longer than usual to look at the ceiling, hesitated, and finally said after a quick glance at Ward, whose eyes were glued to him:

"Because Bessie refused to go any farther."

He looked as if he were saying, "I'm sorry, but it's the truth, and I've sworn to tell the truth and nothing but the truth."

"Bessie did not want to go on as far as Nogales?"

"No, sir."

"Do you know why?"

"I don't know."

"What happened when you all got out of the car?"

Once more Maigret heard the phrase that must have been a military term, latrine duty.

"Did Bessie go off on her own?"

This was the longest examination of the ceiling he had yet made.

"As best I recollect, when she came back she was with Ward."

"Bessie came back?"

"Yes, sir."

"Did she get back in the car?"

"Yes. The car made a U-turn and headed back toward Tucson."

"At what point did Bessie leave the car again?"

"At our second stop. Just after the U-turn, Bessie told Ward she wanted to speak to him."

"From the rear of the car? Beside you?"

"Yes. Sergeant Ward stopped. The two of them got out."

"In which direction did they walk?"

"They took off toward the railroad tracks."

"Were they gone long?"

"Sergeant Ward came back after twenty or twenty-five minutes."

"Did you look at the time?"

"I didn't have my watch on."

"Did he come back alone?"

"Yes. He said, 'To hell with that girl! That'll teach her!' "

"What was he referring to?"

"I don't know, sir."

"Did you find it a natural sort of thing to do to go back to town leaving a woman alone there in the desert?"

He did not answer.

"What did you talk about on your way back?"

"We didn't talk."

"Had you taken along something to drink? Was there a bottle in the car?"

"I don't remember that there was."

"When Ward dropped you in town, opposite the bus depot, did he tell you he was going back to have a look for Bessie?"

"No. He didn't say anything."

"Didn't it seem odd to you that he hadn't taken you three back to the base?"

"It didn't occur to me."

"What did you, Corporal Van Fleet, and Wo Lee do then?"

"We took a taxi."

"What did you talk about then?"

"Nothing."

"Who had decided to take the taxi?"

"I don't know, sir."

"How much time passed between when Ward and Mullins dropped you off and when you took the taxi?"

"Not more'n three minutes. More likely, two."

Really pigheaded kids who obviously had something to hide but from whom nothing had been obtained so far. And why did the inquiry have to be handled in this fashion? Once more Maigret caught himself fidgeting on his bench. And he barely avoided raising his hand, he too behaving like a schoolboy, to ask a question.

He felt himself blush as he caught sight of his colleague Harry Cole in the doorway. How long had he been observing Maigret with his complacent smile? From across the room Cole made the gestures appropriate to ask, "I suppose you'd rather stay?"

After a few moments Cole withdrew on tiptoe, leaving Maigret absorbed in his new passion.

"Where did the taxi leave you off?"

"At the place we'd stopped at the second time."

"At exactly the same place?"

"Because it was dark I can't swear to it. But we tried to remember the exact spot."

Again, "What did you talk about as you were driving out?"

"We didn't talk."

"And you sent the taxi back? How did you expect to get back to town and return to your base?"

"Figured we'd hitch a ride."

"What time was it by then?"

"Must have been about three-thirty."

"You didn't see Ward's car? You didn't see him or Dan Mullins?"

"No, sir."

Ward's eyes never left O'Neil's face and O'Neil tried to avoid his glance. When they made eye contact, O'Neil looked as if he were asking Ward's pardon with the excuse that he was a man forced to do his duty.

"What did you do, the three of you, once you'd been set down on the highway?"

"We walked in the direction of Nogales, then we turned around and walked back toward Tucson, sort of paralleling the railroad tracks."

"Why didn't any of you have the idea of looking on the other side of the highway?"

"I don't know."

"Did you walk a long time?"

"Maybe an hour."

"And you didn't see anybody?"

"No, sir."

"And you didn't talk?"

"No, sir."

"Then what happened?"

"We stopped a car that came along and that took us back to the base."

"Do you know what kind of car it was?"

"No, sir, but I think it was a '46 Chevy."

"Did you talk to the driver?"

"No, sir."

"What did you do when you got back to the base?"

"We all went to sleep. At six, we have to be on deck to check out the planes."

Maigret was boiling. He wanted to shake the little coroner and ask him, "Have you never quizzed a witness in your life? Or are you avoiding asking essential questions on purpose?"

"When did you learn that Bessie Mitchell was dead?"

"When her brother told me, at about five in the afternoon."

"What did he say, exactly?"

"That they'd found Bessie dead on the tracks and that there'd be a coroner's inquest."

"Was anyone else present when Mitchell told you?"

"Yes. Wo Lee was with me in the room. He said, 'I know what happened.' Mitchell started to question him but Wo Lee just told him, 'I'll only tell what I know to the sheriff.' "

It was now a little after five and, with the same abruptness as before, the coroner called for adjournment. He sounded vague, as if thinking of something else, as he mechanically picked up the papers scattered on his desk. "Be here tomorrow at nine-thirty," he said. "Not right *here* but in the second courtroom. That's one floor up."

People were leaving. The five Air Force men gathered outside, still without having spoken a word to each other. A court officer joined them in the corridor and walked them across the patio.

Harry Cole was there, too, in fresh gabardine pants and a white shirt, and wearing the look of a young buck in high good humor.

"So the inquest interests you, Julius? What would you say to a glass of beer?"

Without a break, they found themselves in the broiling heat, in the brightest glare, heat and glare so heavy that sounds seemed muffled. Against the skyline the four or five tall buildings of the city could be seen. People left in their cars—even the Indian. Maigret had learned that he had a wooden leg. He opened the door to an old car whose top was held on with pieces of rope.

"I'll bet you're going to ask me some questions, Julius."

They entered the air-conditioned bar where more pairs of fresh gabardine pants and more white shirts kept company with a line-up of bottles of chilled beer all down the length of the counter. There were cowboys there, too, real ones with their heavy blue denim pants tight to their thighs, their high-heeled boots, and their broad-brimmed hats.

"You're right. If we could put our trip to Nogales off one more day, I'd like to go back to the coroner's inquest tomorrow."

"Here's to you! Don't you have any questions?"

"Of course, lots of them. I'll ask you as they come to mind. Are there any prostitutes around here?"

"Not in your sense of the word. In certain states, yes, they're allowed. But not in Arizona."

"Bessie Mitchell?"

"That's what takes their place."

"Erna Bolton, too?"

"More or less."

"How many soldiers are there at the base?"

"Five or six thousand. I've never bothered to find out exactly."

"A majority of them bachelors?"

"Three-fourths unmarried."

"How do they make out?"

"As best they can. It isn't very easy."

His smile, which seldom left him, was not ironic. He certainly felt respect, perhaps even admiration, for Maigret, whose reputation he was thoroughly familiar with. Still, he was amused to see a Frenchman grappling with problems that were so completely foreign to him.

"I'm from the East, myself," he said, not without a hint of pride. "I come from New England. Here, you see, life's still lived in something of a frontier style. I could have you meet some of the old pioneers who had fought it out with the Apaches at the turn of the century. The very few remaining ones gather once a year and hold court sessions to try any horse thieves or cattle rustlers who've been rounded up."

Not a half hour had passed, and they had already finished three bottles of beer each. Harry Cole decided, "Now it's time for whiskeys!"

Afterwards, they headed for Nogales in the car, and as they drove across Tucson Maigret felt as at sea as he had in the courtroom. This was not a little town, after all, since there were over a hundred thousand inhabitants.

Yet aside from the center of town, where the few buildings of over twenty floors were profiled against the sky like great towers, the rest of Tucson was like a development, or rather like a series of developments juxtaposed to each other. Some were richer, some poorer, but all were made up of equally new, tidy-looking, ranch-style houses.

Farther on, the streets were no longer paved. And there were vast areas where one saw nothing but sand and cactuses. They passed the airport and, without transition, they were in the desert with the great hills violet in the distance.

"This is about where your incident took place! Do you want to get out? Take care to steer clear of the rattlers."

"Are there any?"

"Sometimes you even run across them in town."

The tracks were, in fact, a single track that ran along some fifty yards from the highway.

"I think there are four or five trains a day. Don't you want to lift a glass in Nogales? It's right nearby."

Sixty miles! It's true that they made it in under an hour.

A small town with heavy chain-link fencing and a gate cutting through the main streets. Men in uniform. Harry Cole spoke to them, and an instant later he was plunging with his Julius into a morass of narrow streets, unexpected street noises, everything ill kept, and, over all, a bronze light that seemed out of place.

"We'll begin with the cellars, though it's a bit early."

31

Half-naked boys shoved at each other to get a chance to polish the men's shoes, and grownups detained them at the entrances to their shops, most of which were souvenir shops.

"As you see, it's a fairground. When people from Tucson, or even Phoenix or farther away, want to have a good time, they come here."

And, in fact, in an enormous bar there were only Americans.

"Do you think Bessie Mitchell was killed?"

"I only know that she is dead."

"Accidentally?"

"Now I admit this is none of my business. It's not a federal crime, and I'm only concerned with federal offenses. Everything else belongs to the county authorities." Put differently, it concerned the sheriff and his deputy sheriffs. That was what shocked Maigret most, far more than did this baroque and malodorous fair into the midst of which he and Cole had plunged.

The sheriff, heading up the county constabulary, was not at all a professionally trained public officer moved ahead by advancement within the ranks. Instead, he was a citizen elected to the office much as a municipal councilman might be in Paris. It did not matter what his previous occupation had been. He put in his bid for the nomination and then campaigned to win it.

Once elected, the sheriff chose his deputies—corresponding rather closely to inspectors—pretty much according to personal preference. They were the fellows Maigret had seen with their fancy revolvers and their belts studded with cartridges.

"And that's not all!" Harry Cole had added with ironic emphasis. "There's a whole slew of honorary deputy sheriffs he can name."

"You mean, like me?" Maigret asked, thinking of his silver plaque.

"I'm talking about the sheriff's friends, influential people who helped get him elected. They get the same sort of plaque you did. Nearly all the ranchers are at one time or another deputy sheriffs. And don't think they take this lightly. Why, a few weeks ago a stolen car was being driven by a dangerous convict, an escapee from a nearby prison. He was driving from Tucson toward Nogales. The Tucson sheriff alerted a rancher who lives about midway between the two points. This fellow phoned up two or three of his neighbors, cattle raisers like himself. All of them were deputy sheriffs. They made a roadblock of their own cars across the highway and, when the escaped convict tried to make a run around the end, they fired on his tires. They brought down their quarry, too, whom they ended up by lassoing. Now, what do you think of that?"

Maigret had not had a chance to drink as much as the boys on the witness stand, but the quantity he had ingested was beginning to tell on him. He replied with an amused grumble: "In France, the local people would be more likely to lasso the police!"

He was not sure at exactly what time they got back to Tucson.

Still piloted by Cole, he entered the Penguin Bar about midnight, though he couldn't be perfectly sure of the hour. There was a long counter of dark, polished wood, with multicolored bottles on shelves behind it. Like all bars, the place was suffused with a soft light against which the men's shirts stood out as white patches.

At the back, a vast chrome-plated, imposing jukebox reigned; beside it stood a pinball machine where grown

33

men would stand, for an hour at a time, feeding in coins and maneuvering little metal balls into slots in the hope of winning a free game.

Painted on the box in rather primitive style were bathing beauties. And there was one girl, entirely naked in the style of the *Vie Parisienne* centerfold, on a calendar over the bar.

But real flesh-and-blood women were scarcely to be seen. Two or three of them, at most, were seated in the booths, tables separated from each other by a fixed partition some four to four and a half feet high. These women were all accompanied by men. The couples sat without moving, holding hands, in front of them glasses of beer or whiskey, listening with vague smiles to the music that poured endlessly from the jukebox.

"Aren't we having fun," Maigret commented with a sour laugh.

Cole irritated him, and he could not have explained why. Perhaps it was his eternal know-it-all attitude that put Maigret's nerves on edge.

He was simply an FBI officer who drove a big car with one hand, sometimes even removing that one to light a cigarette while the car sped on at sixty miles an hour. He knew everybody. Everybody knew him. Over the border in Mexico or here, he slapped people on the back, and they would address him affectionately, "Hello, Harry!"

He would introduce Maigret, and they would turn to the Paris Chief Superintendent as if they had always known him, without interest in what he was doing there.

"Have a drink!" they would say.

It didn't matter whether the drink was palatable or not, as long as it could be slugged down.

Here, all along the bar, were men glued to their high

stools, men who did not move except to raise a finger now and then, a gesture the bartender understood perfectly. A few Air Force noncoms drank along with the rest of them. Perhaps there were a few privates, but, if so, Maigret hadn't seen them yet.

"If I understand correctly, they can return to the base at whatever hour they choose. Is that so?"

The question surprised Cole.

"Certainly!"

"At four in the morning, if they wish?"

"So long as they are on deck when they're supposed to be, they don't have to check in at the barracks at all."

"What if they're drunk?"

"That's their business. What counts is for them to do the job."

Why did this infuriate Maigret? Was it because he remembered the ten-o'clock curfew of his own military service, the weeks he would have to wait for one midnight pass?

"Don't forget: it's a volunteer army."

"I know. Where do they recruit them?"

"Wherever they can. In the street. Haven't you seen the trucks that stop sometimes at a crossroads and play records? Inside, there are posters of exotic lands and a sergeant to exlain the advantages of the military life."

Cole always seemed to be playing with life, as if he found it really very amusing.

"You find a little of everything in such a haul, like armies everywhere. I suspect that in France, too, it isn't only the good little boys who go into the army. Hello, Bill! Meet my friend Julius. Have a drink!"

And for the tenth or twentieth time this evening, Maigret heard a perfect stranger tell him his Parisian experiences. Because all these fellows had been to Paris. They all took on a naughty little look to tell him about it.

"Have a drink!"

Suppose the coroner were to ask *him* tomorrow how much he had had to drink! He could now reply truthfully with the rest of them:

"I don't remember exactly. Perhaps twenty drinks?"

The more he drank, the glummer he became until he began to take on Sergeant O'Neil's pigheaded look.

He had decided to understand this scene, and understand it he would! That's all there was to it! He had already discovered why Harry Cole irritated him so. The FBI man was convinced that Maigret might be a bigwig in his own country but that here, in the United States, he could not figure out what was what.

The more Cole watched him puzzle things out, the more amused he became. Well, Maigret held strictly to the belief that men were everywhere the same, moved by the same passions.

What it took was a conscious disregard for the superficial differences: one should not be amazed, for example, at the height of the buildings, at the desert, the cactuses, the cowboy boots, the pinball machines, the jukeboxes.

"There were five fellows and one girl. So far so good. And all but one of them had been drinking." They had been drinking as Maigret was now, automatically, just as the men were doing all up and down the bar.

"Hello! Harry!"

"Hello, Jim!"

Would you believe that nobody had a family name? Would you believe that they were all on a footing of close friendship? Each time Cole introduced him, he would

36

add in a meaningful aside, "A wonderful guy!" Or perhaps, "A first-rate fellow!"

Never did he say, in a really low tone, "This one's a stinker."

Where were the stinkers? Did this mean there weren't any? Or did it mean, simply, that here they were more tolerant?

"Do you think the five Air Force men are free to come and go in the evening?"

"Why wouldn't they be?"

What they'd have drawn in Paris! And especially how they would have been treated each time they came back to the base!

"Nothing's been proved against them, after all."

"Not yet," Maigret grouched.

"Until a man has been found guilty . . ."

"I know! I know! . . ."

He drained his glass and felt in a thoroughly ill humor. Then he looked back at the couples. In some cases, their mouths had been glued together for upwards of five minutes and the men's hands were not to be seen.

"Tell me, these couples are probably not married?"

"No, probably not."

"So they have no right to go to a hotel?"

"Not unless they sign in as husband and wife, a crime of perjury that could have dire consequences, particularly if they come from out of state."

"Where can they go to make love?"

"What's to say that later on they'll still need to make love, as you put it?"

Maigret shrugged furiously.

"And then, there's always the car."

"What if they don't have a car?"

37

"That's unlikely. Most people have a car. If they don't have one, they cope as best they can. After all, it's their business, isn't it?"

"What if they were caught making love on the street or highway?"

"That would cost them a pretty penny!"

"And what if the girl were seventeen and a half instead of eighteen?"

"It could land her partner in jail for up to ten years."

"But Bessie Mitchell was not yet eighteen."

"She had been married and divorced."

"What about Maggie Wallach, the musician's mistress . . . ?"

"What makes you think so?"

"Seems obvious."

"Did you ever see them at it?"

Maigret ground his teeth.

"Besides, note that *she*'s been married and divorced."

"What about Erna Bolton, the one who's with the brother?"

"She's twenty."

"I see you know the dossier."

"Me? It's none of my business. I've already told you that I can only deal with federal offenses. If they had made use of the postal services, for instance, in order to perpetrate a crime, that would fall into my bailiwick. Or if they'd smoked as much as a single joint of marijuana Have a drink, Julius!"

There were some twenty men lined up at the counter, drinking and staring straight ahead of them at the line-up of bottles and the calendar featuring the naked woman. There were naked or near-naked women portrayed almost everywhere, in the ads, on the publicity calendars; there were photographs of pretty girls in bathing suits on every page in the newspapers, on every movie screen.

"But what the hell happens to these men when they want a woman?"

Harry Cole, who could handle his whiskey better than Maigret, looked him straight in the eye and burst out laughing. "They get married!"

So it was really on purpose that the coroner had not asked the most elementary-seeming questions! How could he hope to get at the truth in this fashion? Or was the whole thing a big game?

Perhaps, after all, the coroner's inquest was only a mere formality, and no one really cared too much to find out what had happened that night.

One of the two men who had testified until now was clearly lying. Either it was Sergeant Ward or it was Sergeant O'Neil.

No one seemed surprised at this. Each was interrogated with the same degree of courtesy, or rather with the same detachment.

"Could the barman be called on to testify?"

"Whatever for?"

It was the same man who served them this evening, the bartender with the head of a boxer.

"They're going to put us out at any moment," Cole said, looking at his watch. "Do you want to pick up anything to take with us?"

And, as Maigret looked at him in surprise, Cole pointed out two of the clients who had stopped at another counter on the way out to buy alcohol by the bottle. They paid and slipped pints into their back pockets.

"Perhaps they have a long way to drive. Or they have trouble getting to sleep. That must be it."

The FBI man chuckled to himself, and Maigret did not

say another word until Cole let him off in front of the Pioneer Hotel.

"If I get the picture, you're spending tomorrow in court?"

Maigret grunted a vague reply.

"I'll pick you up in time for lunch. You're in luck. The morning session takes place in the second chamber, a flight up. It's air-conditioned. Good night, Julius!"

And he added without malice, as if he were not talking about a dead girl, "Don't dream of Bessie, now!"

3

The Little Chinese
Who Did Not Drink

At least three people said good morning when Maigret
turned up in court the following day, and this pleased
him. The second floor of the county courthouse was surrounded by an arcade just like the one on the ground
floor. The sun was already hot, and groups of men smoked
their cigarettes in the shade while they awaited Ezekiel's
summons.

Ezekiel in particular, his fat pipe in his mouth, had
given Maigret a cordial greeting, as had the juror with the
wooden leg.

He had asked himself, as he came along from his hotel,
if the public's attitude toward Sergeant Ward might have
changed noticeably.

Yesterday afternoon, when O'Neil spoke of the second
time the car had stopped and stated that Ward and Bessie
had walked together in the direction of the railroad
tracks, there had been not an audible response but something like a little collective shock. Everyone must have
felt more or less the same reaction, like a blow between
the ribs.

41

Were they going to look at Ward now as men involuntarily do when they know that one among them has killed someone?

The five servicemen were there, not far from the officer who had escorted them. They stood about smoking, like the others, while waiting to be called inside. Like sullen schoolboys, they kept a certain distance among themselves.

It seemed to Maigret that Ward, very blue eyes under thick black brows, kept a bit more to himself than did the others and that from a slight distance people outside the Air Force group cast furtive glances at him.

Had he gone home to sleep overnight at his own house? What was his attitude now toward his wife? And what was her attitude? Had he begged her pardon? Had they quarreled once and for all?

The young Chinese with his great almond-shaped eyes was as delicate and pretty as a girl. Small of stature, he seemed much younger than the others. In schools, too, there is always one whom the big boys tease by calling him a sissy.

There were a few new curious spectators. The newspaper had come out with an account of the first day's hearing under fat headlines:

SERGEANT WARD CLAIMS HE WAS DRUGGED
O'NEIL CONTRADICTS HIS TESTIMONY
ON SEVERAL POINTS

O'Neil still looked to Maigret like the conscientious pupil, top of the class. Too conscientious. Had he and Ward exchanged as much as a word since the day before?

Maigret had awakened in a foul humor, his head aching and, if the truth were known, with a first-rate hangover,

42

but it had all passed. Just the same, he had been irritated to have to adopt their system. From his first days in New York he had been amazed to see men whom he had left the night before in a state of advanced drunkenness all fresh-faced and, as they said, rarin' to go the next morning. Then someone had told him their secret. After that, he noted in all the drugstores, in cafés, in bars, the special blue bottle mounted on a wall bracket, its spout down, out of which the proper dose of effervescent powder could be measured. Dropped into a glass to which the barman added water, the compound fizzed and tingled. This was served you as promptly as a morning coffee or a Coca-Cola, and a few minutes after ingesting it the fumes of the alcohol had been dispersed.

Yet why not? Machines for getting drunk, machines for getting over being drunk. They were logical people, after all.

"Gentlemen of the jury . . . jurors!"

Everyone entered the classroom, and this one was quite a lot larger than that of the day before. This time it even seemed to be a real courtroom with a balustrade like the sort at which one takes Communion acting as a barrier between court and public; there was a chair for the coroner and a desk furnished with a microphone for the witness. The jurors, now seated in a regular jury box, seemed more solemn in these surroundings.

In fact, Maigret noticed more attentively people he had only caught sight of the day before, among others a thick-set red-haired man who stayed close to the attorney, taking notes and occasionally talking to him in low tones. At first Maigret had taken him for a secretary or a newspaperman.

"Who's that?" he asked his neighbor.

"Mike."

The Superintendent knew that, since he'd heard other people call him by his first name.

"What's he do?"

"Mike O'Rourke? He's the chief deputy sheriff. He's the one in charge of the inquest."

The county Maigret, in short. They were about equally stout, had the same spare tire above their belts, the same stocky necks, and they must have been of about the same age.

Was it, after all, so different here from Paris? O'Rourke did not wear his sheriff's badge and did not carry a pistol thrust into a holster at his waist. He looked like a calm sort of fellow, with the very fair complexion of redheads, and violet eyes.

Was it he who proposed the next question to the attorney, over whom he often leaned? Whether it was or no, as soon as the session opened, the attorney rose and asked permission to address a question to yesterday's last witness. Thus O'Neil went to sit at the desk beside the microphone, which they adjusted to his height.

"Did you notice the condition of the car in which you returned to Tucson? Wasn't it damaged?"

The good pupil knitted his brows and raised his eyes questioningly to the ceiling.

"I don't know."

"Was it a two-door or a four-door car? Did you get in on the right or the left?"

"I think it was a four-door. I got in on the side opposite the driver."

"So you got in on the right. And you didn't notice that the body was dented, as if the car had been in an acci dent?"

"I don't remember anymore."

44

"Were you very drunk by then?"

"Yes, sir."

"Were you more drunk than when Bessie left the group?"

"I don't know. Maybe."

"Yet you hadn't had anything more to drink since you'd left the musician's house?"

"That's right, sir."

"That's all."

O'Neil got up.

"Pardon me, one more question. Where were you sitting in this last car?"

"I sat in front, beside the driver."

The attorney indicated that he had no more questions, and it was now Van Fleet's turn. This sergeant was a blond young man with wavy hair and a brick-red tan. In his own mind, Maigret had dubbed him the Dutchman. His pals called him Pinky.

He was the first who clearly showed that he was nervous as he took his seat in the jury box. He made a visible effort to calm down, but he didn't know which way to look and more than once he sat biting his nails.

"Are you married or a bachelor?"

"Bachelor, sir."

He had to cough to clear his throat so that he could be heard, and the coroner turned up the microphone. The coroner had been given a truly remarkable chair: it could be made to hold a variety of positions and the man spent his time lowering the back little by little, then bringing it a bit forward, then lowering it once more.

"Tell us what happened on July 27 from seven-thirty in the evening on."

Behind Maigret, a young black woman with a baby in arms whom he had noticed the day before had come with her brother and sister. There were two pregnant women in the courtroom. Thanks to the air conditioning, it was cool, much cooler than it had been downstairs. Nonetheless, Ezekiel went to fiddle with the apparatus from time to time, self-importantly.

The Fleming talked slowly, with long silences during which he seemed to be searching for words. The four other soldiers, seated on the single witness bench, had their backs to the public, and it was at them that Pinky stole furtive glances, as if begging them to prompt him.

The Penguin Bar, the musician's apartment, the take-off for Nogales . . .

"Where were you seated in Ward's car?"

"At first, I was in back with Corporal Wo Lee and Sergeant O'Neil, but I had to move in front when Ward told Bessie to change places. Then I sat to Mullins's right."

"What happened then?"

"After the airport, the car stopped on the right-hand side of the road, and we all got out."

"Had you all decided by then not to go on to Nogales?"
"No."

"When did that come up?"

"When everybody got back into the car."

"Including Bessie?"

He hesitated, and it seemed to Maigret that his eyes sought out O'Neil.

"Yes. Ward said we were heading back to town."

"Bessie didn't mention it?"

"I heard Ward say it."

"Did the car stop a second time?"

"Yes. Bessie told Ward she wanted to talk to him."

"Was she very drunk? Was she still aware of what she was doing?"

"I think she was. They went off together."

46

"How long were they gone?"

"Ward came back alone after five or six minutes."

"You say five or six minutes? Did you look at the time?"

"No. But I don't think he stayed away longer than that."

"What did he say then?"

"He didn't say anything."

"Didn't anybody ask him what had happened to Bessie?"

"No, sir."

"Didn't it seem strange to you that you were all leaving without her?"

"Maybe a little."

"Didn't Ward say anything at all on the way back?"

"No, sir."

"Who decided to take a taxi to go back to the spot you'd last stopped?"

He indicated O'Neil with a gesture.

"Didn't you and O'Neil argue about whether or not to take Wo Lee with you?"

Maigret, who had nearly dozed off, started awake. This was a little, inconspicuous question that seemed to him to indicate that the coroner was much more with it than he wished to appear. O'Rourke was leaning close to the ear of the attorney, who was taking notes.

"No, sir."

"What did you talk about on the way back?"

"We didn't talk."

"When the taxi stopped, wasn't there any . . . discussion between you and O'Neil?"

"I don't remember any. No, sir."

O'Rourke must have known his business. He had located the taxi driver, which couldn't have been hard to do, and in due course they would hear him give his testimony.

Of the three soldiers questioned until now, Pinky was by far the most ill at ease.

"Aren't you and O'Neil roommates? How long have you been rooming together?"

"For about six months."

"Aren't you very close friends?"

"We always go out together."

When the prosecuting attorney was asked if he had any questions to address to the witness, he asked only one.

"Was the car that brought you back to the base in good condition?"

Pinky could not tell, either. He had not noticed the make of the car and remembered only that the body color was either white or very light.

"Session adjourned!"

How strange it was—Sergeant Ward already seemed less of a murderer. Now it was O'Neil whom people stared at in the corridors. Perhaps he was perfectly innocent. Perhaps they were all innocent. And they felt suspicion travel from one of them to the other. Perhaps they even suspected one another?

What were they thinking as they smoked their cigarettes on the balconies and drank their Coca-Colas?

Maigret could have introduced himself to O'Rourke, who would have clapped him on the shoulder and who might have shared his professional secrets with him. But he was more intrigued to watch the comings and goings of his opposite number, who took advantage of the adjournment to go into an adjacent, glassed-in office to make a few phone calls.

When the trial resumed, it was apparent that the prosecuting attorney was still missing, so he had to be looked for throughout the building. Perhaps he too had gone to make a few phone calls.

"Corporal Wo Lee."

The witness slid into the chair and the microphone was lowered to the height of his mouth. He spoke in so low a tone that he could scarcely be heard despite the amplifier.

The three who had already testified had taken their time between phrases. But Wo Lee took so long that one might have thought he had broken down completely or had suddenly decided to think about something else.

Was it that like a band of schoolboys who had done something truly naughty, they were privately accusing each other of having ratted?

Maigret had to lean forward and pay the strictest attention, for the young Chinese was hard for him to follow.

"Tell us what happened on the . . ."

The recital was so slow that before he had reached his version of the departure for Nogales, the coroner had once more adjourned. During the break three prisoners in blue uniforms were brought in, people whom the police had picked up the day before and who had nothing to do with the case at hand.

A Mexican of markedly Indian origin was accused of drunkenness and of disrupting the peace on the main roads.

"Do you plead guilty?"

"Yes."

"Five-dollar fine or five days in prison. Next!"

A bounced check.

"Do you plead guilty? We'll hold your hearing over to August 7. You'll be released on bail of five hundred dollars."

Maigret went downstairs to drink a Coca-Cola, and two of the jurors smiled at him as he went by. He had to cross a sunny patch of the balcony and felt the great heat like a burn on his skin.

49

When he came back, the Chinese was once more in the witness chair and was starting to answer a question he had just been asked.

There were now people standing in the open doorway but no one had taken Maigret's seat, which pleased him.

"As we were leaving the bar, we bought two bottles of whiskey," Wo Lee said slowly.

"What happened at the musician's apartment?"

"Bessie and Sergeant Mullins went into the kitchen. A little later, Sergeant Ward went in there too and they had an argument."

"Between the two men or between Bessie and Ward?"

"I don't know. Ward came back with a bottle in his hand."

"Had the two bottles been drunk?"

"No. One had been left in the car."

"On the seat in front or on the seat in back?"

"On the seat in back."

"On which side?"

"On the left side."

"Who was seated on the left?"

"Sergeant O'Neil."

"Did you see him take a drink as you all were driving along?"

"It was too dark for me to see."

"During the evening, did Harold Mitchell seem mad at his sister?"

"No, sir."

Today Bessie's brother was in uniform. Yesterday, in civvies and wearing a shirt of a particularly lurid violet, he had looked like a film tough guy. But today, in clean and freshly pressed poplin, he seemed more open. At a certain point while the Chinese was speaking, the musician, who had been outside, came in to find Mitchell and then talked to him briefly in a low voice on the balcony. When Mitchell returned, he went to Mike O'Rourke who, in turn, spoke to the prosecutor. The attorney rose:

"Sergeant Mitchell asks that a witness be called as soon as possible."

Sergeant Mitchell was seated, as he had been the day before, beside Maigret. He got up when the coroner turned toward him and said, his voice trembling:

"The word's out that some of the trainmen saw a piece of rope around my sister's wrist. I'd like to hear what they have to say."

He was given a sign that he could sit down again; the coroner spoke to his bailiff and then resumed his interrogation.

"What happened when the car stopped about a mile beyond the airport?"

Once more they were treated to the phrase "latrine duty" but this time spoken with a different accent, which automatically brought a smile to people's lips as if it had been a gag.

"Did you see Bessie walk away from the car?"

"Yes. She went off with Sergeant Mullins."

People now stared at Mullins's back, and Ward became less and less of a murderer.

"Were they gone a long time? Where was Ward during that time?"

"He was one of the first to come back to the car. Then Bessie got in and we had to wait for Mullins for several minutes."

"How long were Bessie and Mullins together?"

"Perhaps ten minutes."

"Had they already decided not to go on to Nogales?"

"No. It was when we were about to take off again that Bessie said she'd had enough and wanted to go home."

"Ward turned around toward Tucson without a pro-test?"

"Yes, sir."

"Tell us what happened then. You hadn't had anything to drink all evening long, had you?"

"Only Coca-Cola. After a few yards Bessie asked him to stop the car again."

"Did she say anything else?"

"No."

"Who got out of the car with her?"

"Nobody, at first. She went off on her own. Then Dan Mullins got out of the car, too."

"You're sure it was Mullins?"

"Yes, sir."

"Did he stay a long time?"

"At least ten minutes, maybe longer."

"Did he go toward the railroad?"

"Yes. Then Sergeant Ward got out on the left-hand side and walked all around the car. He came back almost at once because we heard Mullins's footsteps."

"Did the two men have an argument?"

"No. The car started off. They let us out in front of the bus depot, Sergeant O'Neil, Van Fleet, and me."

"Who suggested you go back?"

"Sergeant O'Neil."

"Did they ask you not to go back with them?"

"Not exactly. O'Neil simply asked me if I wasn't too tired and if I wouldn't rather go back to the base."

"What was said in the taxi?"

"Van Fleet and O'Neil talked low in the back seat. I was in front with the driver and I didn't listen."

"Who told the driver where to stop?"

"O'Neil."

"Was it the spot where you'd first stopped or was it the second?"

"I can't tell you. It was still dark."

"Was there any discussion at this point?"

"No, sir."

"Did the question arise of whether or not to have the taxi wait?"

The question had not come up. They had gone to look for a girl left stranded in the desert, and they had not kept the car to take them back to town.

"Did you meet or pass any other cars along the highway?"

"No, sir."

"What did you do once the taxi had left?"

"We walked in the direction of Nogales; then, after about a mile, we turned around."

"All together?"

"On the way out, yes. On the way back, I walked along the edge of the road. Sergeant O'Neil and Pinky walked farther out in the desert."

"On the side of the road where the railroad tracks are?"

"Yes, sir."

"How long did these goings and comings take?"

"About an hour."

"And during that hour you didn't see anyone? You didn't hear any train? What color was the car that brought you back?"

"Pale yellow."

The attorney rose to put the question to which he seemed to attach particular, inexplicable importance.

"Did you notice if the body of the car gave any signs of having been in an accident?"

"No, sir. I got in on the right-hand side."

"What about O'Neil?"

"He did, too. It was a sedan. He sat in front and I behind. Pinky went around."

"Was the bottle of whiskey still with you?"

"No."

"Was it with you when you were in the taxi?"

"I'm not sure. I don't think so."

"Next day, when Harold Mitchell told you that his sister had been killed, you told him that you knew what had happened but that you would only talk in front of the sheriff."

Maigret saw Mitchell's hand clench on his knee.

"No, sir."

"Didn't you speak with him?"

"I told him, 'The sheriff will ask us questions and I'll tell him what I know.' "

This was clearly not the same thing, and Mitchell, sitting beside Maigret, made a nervous gesture of vexation, even anger.

Was the young Chinese lying? Which one of the four of them who had been heard until now had been lying?

"Session adjourned! We will resume downstairs, in the room of the Justice of the Peace, in an hour and a half."

Harry Cole was not there as he had promised to be, and Maigret saw him get out of his car a little later in front of the county courthouse. He was as fresh-looking and alert as he had been the day before, and his infallible good humor seemed to well up out of him as if from an inexhaustible source. It was the kind of serene good spirits that characterize a man who has no bad dreams, a man who feels at peace with himself and with others.

They were pretty much all like that, and that was what put Maigret off.

It made him think of too tidy a garment, too well

washed and pressed. Their houses were like that, too, just as impeccable as good hospitals where there was no reason to sit down in one corner rather than another.

He suspected that, at bottom, they suffered the same anxieties as the rest of humanity but that they assumed this happy-go-lucky appearance out of embarrassment.

Even the five men in the Air Force were not sufficiently troubled, he felt. Each fellow was shut up in himself, but without one's being able to sense any of that inner stress people feel who, rightly or wrongly, are suspected of a crime.

The spectators, too, seemed unperturbed. No one appeared to be thinking of that girl who had died on the railroad track. It was more like a sort of game to which the reporter of the *Star* had only to add the titillating headlines.

"Did you sleep well, Julius?"

If only they wouldn't call him Julius! The worst of it was they didn't even do it on purpose; there was no irony in it for them.

"Have you resolved the problem? Was it a crime, a suicide, or an accident?"

Maigret turned into the corner bar as if it were home. There he recognized several faces from the audience, including those of two jurors.

"Have a drink! You had a case somewhat like this in France, didn't you? Some member of a town council was found on a railroad track. What was his name?"

"Prince," Maigret growled.

And the case hit him hard all over again for there, too, the victim had been found with a rope around his wrists.

"How did it wind up?"

"It hasn't been wound up yet."

"But you have your own ideas?"

He had, but he preferred not to discuss the matter further, since his views had already caused him enough trouble and even attacks from a segment of the press.

"Did you have a chance to shoot the breeze with Mike? You know each other, don't you? He's the chief deputy sheriff and he deals personally with things of any real importance. Shouldn't I introduce you?"

"Not right now."

"Well, in that case, let's go eat a steak and onions; then I'll drop you off at the county courthouse in plenty of time."

"Aren't you following the case at all?"

"I've told you, this isn't my bailiwick."

"But doesn't it interest you, either?"

"One can't be interested in everything, right? If I do Mike O'Rourke's work, who will do mine? Maybe today or tomorrow I'll get my hands on a big stash of dope that's been in the area for upwards of a week."

"How do you know?"

"One of our agents in Mexico. I even know who sold it, what he got for the package, and what day the transaction took place. I know when the stuff crossed the border at Nogales. I even think I know in whose truck it was brought to Tucson. After that, I'm all at sea."

The waitress at the cafeteria was fresh-looking and pretty. She was a well-stacked blonde, about twenty years old.

Cole greeted her, "Hello, Doll!"

And to Maigret he added, "She's a student at the university. She's hoping to get a scholarship for a year's study in Paris."

Why did Chief Inspector Maigret feel an urge to be crude the minute he was with Harry Cole?

56

"What if I pinched her bottom?" he asked, thinking of the girls who waited tables at the little bistros in France.

His American colleague seemed surprised, gave him a long look, and appeared to be considering the question seriously.

"I don't know," he finally admitted. "You could try. Doll!"

Did he really expect Maigret to stretch out his hand while the young girl bent over them, her white uniform stretched taut by the firm, healthy flesh beneath?

"Sergeant Mullins!"

Another bachelor. Ward was the only one in the whole batch who was married and had children.

Didn't that make Dan Mullins something of a villainous figure under the present circumstances?

"Tell us what happened on the night of . . ."

Maigret preferred the smaller room on the ground floor to the one upstairs, despite the greater heat. It was more intimate, and Ezekiel, here where he felt right at home, behaved in a more characteristic fashion.

He was the school patrol. The coroner was the headmaster, and the prosecuting attorney was a visiting superintendent.

Would they ever get down to asking the essential questions? Sergeant Ward had already admitted that he had been jealous of his friend Mullins. And it was in the latter's company that he had come upon Bessie in the musician's kitchen.

Yet once more they evaded the basics. Five men and a girl had spent a good part of the night together. All except for the young Chinese were loaded with liquor. Four out of five were bachelors, and Maigret now knew what slender chances they had to satisfy their desires. As for Ward, who seemed a jealous type, it looked as if he had Bessie under his skin.

Yet not a word. Always the sempiternal questions. The coroner himself must have attached so little importance to them that he asked them without even looking at the witness. More often than not, he looked up at the ceiling. Did he so much as listen to the answers?

There was only Mike O'Rourke, the county Maigret, who took notes and seemed interested in the case. The black woman, behind the Chief Inspector, had given her baby the breast and her retinue had been increased by the arrival of a little girl and a fat woman. If the inquiry went on long enough, the entire tribe would file into the courtroom.

"Had you met Bessie before?"

"Once, sir."

"Alone?"

"I was with Ward when he first met her at the drive-in. I left them when they went off in the car, about three A.M."

"Did you know Sergeant Ward intended to get a divorce to marry her?"

"No, sir."

And that was all he was asked on that point.

"What happened when the car stopped a little after you'd passed the airport?"

"We all got out. I went off on my own for ..."

By now they had all come to expect the phrase "latrine duty"! The picture of five men and a woman scattered at random near the car and voiding all the liquid they had ingested during the night began to take on an obsessional quality.

"Did you go off by yourself?"

"Yes, sir."

"Did you see Sergeant Ward?"

"I saw him disappear into the darkness with Bessie."

"Did they come back together?"

"Ward came back and sat once more in the driver's seat. Then he snapped, impatiently: 'To hell with that girl! That'll teach her!'"

"Excuse me, but did Ward say that during the first stop?"

"Yes, sir. There was no other stop before Tucson."

"Didn't Bessie ask Ward to go with her because she wanted to speak to him alone?"

"Yes, earlier."

"Earlier than what?"

"Just at the instant the car stopped. It was she who said she didn't want to go any farther, and Ward slowed down. Then she added, 'I have to talk to you. Come.'"

"At the first stop?"

"There wasn't any other stop."

The silence was rather a long one. The backs of the four other soldiers were motionless. The coroner sighed.

"And then what happened?"

"We got back to town and we dropped off the three others."

"Why did you stay with Ward?"

"Because he asked me to."

"When?"

"I don't remember."

"Did he tell you he intended to go back and look for Bessie?"

"No, but that's what I understood."

"Did you give him any cigarettes?"

59

"No. As he was driving, he asked me to get his pack out of his shirt pocket. I took a cigarette out of it and lit it for him."

"Was it a Chesterfield?"

"No, sir, a Camel. There were three or four left in the pack."

"Did you smoke too?"

"I don't think so. I fell asleep."

"Before the car stopped?"

"I think so, or immediately after. When Ward woke me, I saw a telegraph pole and a cactus near the car."

"Did neither of you get out of the car?"

"I don't know if Ward did. I was asleep. He took me over to his place and heaved a pillow at me so I could sleep on his couch."

"Did you see his wife?"

"Not then. I heard them talking, though."

"To sum it up, then, you went back over that same road to look for Bessie and you didn't get out of the car."

"That's right, sir."

"Did you see any other cars? Did you hear the train?"

"No, sir."

All these big, strong fellows were between eighteen and twenty-three. Bessie, who had been seventeen, had married, had been divorced, and was now dead.

"Session adjourned!"

As he passed the glassed-in office, Maigret heard the attorney talking into the telephone.

"Yes, Doctor. In a few minutes. Thank you. We'll wait. . . ."

No doubt he had been talking to the doctor who had performed the autopsy and who would be the next witness. He must have been very busy because the break between sessions lasted more than a half hour. This gave

60

the coroner time to dispose of five or six ordinary delin-quents.

In a corner of the corridor, the attorney and Mike O'Rourke were having a heated discussion, and they called in for consultation the officer who had the five men in his custody. Soon after, they closeted themselves in the office marked PRIVATE, where the coroner joined them.

4

The Man Who
Wound Clocks

One of Maigret's uncles, his mother's brother, had a mania. As soon as he entered a room with a clock in it—no matter what type of clock, little or big, an antique with weights under a glass dome or a mantelpiece alarm clock —he stopped listening to the conversation until he could finally draw near enough the clock to wind it.

He did this wherever he went, even when visiting people he hardly knew. He had been known to do the same in stores where he had gone, to buy a pencil, perhaps, or some nails.

Yet he was not a watchmaker; he worked for the Bureau of the Registry.

Did Maigret take after his uncle? Cole had left him a note at the hotel desk and with it a flat key in the envelope.

Dear Julius,
  Must take a flying leap over to Mexico by plane. Will probably be back by tomorrow morning. You'll

find my car in the hotel parking lot. Here's the key.

Faithfully yours . . .

What would Cole have thought of him, what would he have thought of the French police, if he had known that Maigret had never learned to drive?

Here, men of his age piloted their own planes. The ranchers who are, after all, no more than large-scale farmers, nearly all had their own planes which they used on Sundays to go fishing. In addition, many of them used helicopters to spray their crops.

He did not want to eat dinner alone in the hotel dining room, so he started out on foot. He had long yearned to tramp the streets, but no one ever gave him a chance to do it. As they themselves said, to go two blocks—a distance of two large house lots—they would jump into their cars.

He passed a handsome Colonial type of mansion whose white columns rose, flanking a well-kept lawn. Last evening he had noticed the neon sign CAROON MORTUARY. This was the local funeral parlor. "The Best Funeral at the Best Price" was their newspaper slogan.

And every evening Caroon Mortuary sponsored half an hour of sweet music over the radio. It was there they embalmed people. Acquaintances had looked at Maigret with ill-concealed distaste when he had mentioned that, in France, the dead were returned to earth without having been cleaned out like fish or chickens.

The little doctor, a dry, nervous type who seemed in a frantic hurry, had not said much at the coroner's inquest. He had described the head as "completely scalped," the arms as having been cut off, and the flesh as having been "flung about, helter-skelter."

"Could you determine the cause of death?"

"It was certainly caused by the impact of the locomotive. The top of the skull had been severed like the lid snapped off a box, and fragments of human brain were found several yards away."

"Do you declare that Bessie was alive when she was struck by the train?"

"Yes, sir."

"Could she not have been unconscious, either due to a blow received earlier or to the results of intoxication?"

"It is quite possible."

"Did you find any trace of blows that could have been the cause of death?"

"Any such findings would have been impossible, given the state of the corpse."

And that was all. No reference to the examination of more intimate parts that must have been made.

Maigret was pretty much the only walker along the sidewalks here in the center of the city; this had also been true of all the other American cities he had stopped in. No one lives in the heart of the city. As soon as the offices and shops close, most people stream back to the residential areas, leaving the streets nearly empty. Yet the lights in the store windows stay on all night.

He passed by a drive-in and suddenly wanted to stop for a hot dog. Half a dozen cars, parked in front of the service pass-through, fanned out while two young girls waited on their occupants. There was a counter of a sort inside, with stools anchored to the floor, but he thought it looked cheap to arrive on foot and sit inside.

This impression that he was acting like a cheapskate hit him several times a day. These people had everything. In no matter what town, the cars were as numerous and as streamlined as along the Champs-Elysées. And everyone wore new clothes, new shoes. Cobblers must be unheard-of. And everyone looked scrubbed within an inch of his life and prosperous.

The houses were new too, filled with the latest gadgets. They had everything, that was the word.

Yet five stout fellows, averaging twenty years each, had been brought up before the coroner because they had spent the night drinking with a girl who was later torn to shreds by a train.

What could it matter to him? He wasn't here, after all, to worry about such things. The study-research trips like the one he had been offered after so many years' work were more like perks than right and proper study. He just had to roll with it as they took him from city to city, accept their good dinners, their whiskeys, their cocktails, their plaques making him deputy sheriff. And, of course, he had to listen to their stories.

Yet he could not resist. He found himself as much a prey to anxiety as when, in France, he was involved in some complicated case that he was supposed to unravel, at whatever cost.

O.K. So they had everything. Yet the newspapers were filled with reports of crimes of all kinds. They had just arrested in Phoenix a gang of thugs, the oldest of whom was fifteen and the youngest, twelve. In Texas, an eighteen-year-old student, already married, had killed his wife's sister. A thirteen-year-old married "woman" had just given birth to twins while her husband was in jail for robbery.

Mechanically, he turned toward the Penguin Bar. When he had been driven over the same route, he had thought it just a few blocks away. On foot, he had a more accurate impression of the vastness of the place, and he began to regret not having taken a taxi, for now he was perspiring.

They had everything. So why were those people who sat at the Penguin Bar from opening till closing time so downcast?

Was Maigret like his uncle, then, the one who wound clocks including those that didn't belong to him? It was the first time he had thought of his uncle in this way and perhaps, in so doing, he had discovered the real reason why that otherwise unexceptional man had the mania he did. He must have had a phobia against clocks that had run down. Now a properly running clock can stop at any given moment. People are careless, they forget to wind their clocks.

It was instinctive: he did it for them.

Maigret too felt uneasy when something or someone did not seem to him to be functioning properly. Then he would try to understand, poke his nose into unlikely places, sniff about.

What was it that did not function properly in this country where they have everything?

The men were big and strong, in robust health, clean and rather upbeat in general. The women were nearly all pretty. The stores bulged with goods of every kind, and the houses were planned for people's every comfort; movie theaters were on every other corner, or so it seemed; a beggar was never to be seen, and misery seemed unknown.

The funeral director paid for a radio music program, and the cemeteries were such lovely parks that one felt no impulse to see them surrounded by high walls with gates that locked, as if one should be afraid of the dead.

People's homes, too, were set amid lawns, and, at this hour, men in shirt sleeves or stripped to the waist could be seen watering the grass and flowers. There were no fences or hedges to separate the gardens from one another.

They had everything, all right! They organized themselves almost scientifically so that life would be as agreeable as possible. From the moment the alarm went off in the morning, your radio affectionately wished you a good day in the name of your favorite breakfast cereal, without even forgetting your birthday when it came.

Then what was amiss?

It was this question, he decided, that bound him to those five men whom he didn't know from Adam, and to Bessie, of whom he hadn't even seen a decent photograph, wretched little dead Bessie, and to the other characters he saw take their turn on the stand at the inquest.

Many things differ from one country to another; some things are the same the world over.

But perhaps what changes most across the borders is misery.

The misery of the poor quarters of Paris, of the little bistros around the Porte d'Italie or Saint-Ouen, the filthy wretchedness of the Zone and the more decent wretchedness of Montmartre or Père-Lachaise were all familiar to him. The bottom-line misery of the piers, too, of Place Maubert or the Salvation Army.

All that is misery one can understand, whose origins are known and whose scenario one can follow.

But here he guessed at the existence of a misery without tatters, cleanly, wretchedness with bathrooms, which seemed to him even harsher, more implacable, more desperate.

At last, he pushed open the door to the Penguin Bar and hitched himself up on a bar stool. The bartender, remembering what he had been drinking the night before, asked him cordially, "Manhattan?"

He said yes. It was all the same to him. It was only eight in the evening and night had not really fallen, yet there were already some twenty people lined up at the bar and a few tables in the booths were occupied.

A young girl wearing slacks and a white blouse was waiting tables. He had not noticed her before. He followed her with his eyes. Her pants of thin black gabardine clung to her hips and thighs at each step. She looked as if she had stepped out of an ad or off some calendar or film poster.

When she finished serving people, she slipped a coin in the jukebox and chose a sentimental tune. Then she came to lean her elbows on one end of the bar and dream.

There were no outdoor terraces where one could sit and sip an apéritif, watching the passers-by in the waning sunlight and breathing the scent of the chestnut trees.

People drank, but to do so they had to shut themselves away in these closed-off bars, as if they were fulfilling some shameful need.

Was this, perhaps, why they drank so much?

The railway mechanic had been questioned last. He was a well-dressed fellow, neither young nor old, whom Maigret had first taken for some sort of official.

"When I first saw the body, it was too late to stop the train. We were hauling sixty-eight loaded freight cars behind us."

Fruit and vegetables came in from Mexico in refrigerated cars. Goods arrived from every country in the world. Hundreds of cargo boats docked at the ports daily.

They had everything.

"Was it day already?" the attorney had asked.

"It was beginning to grow light. She was stretched across the track."

68

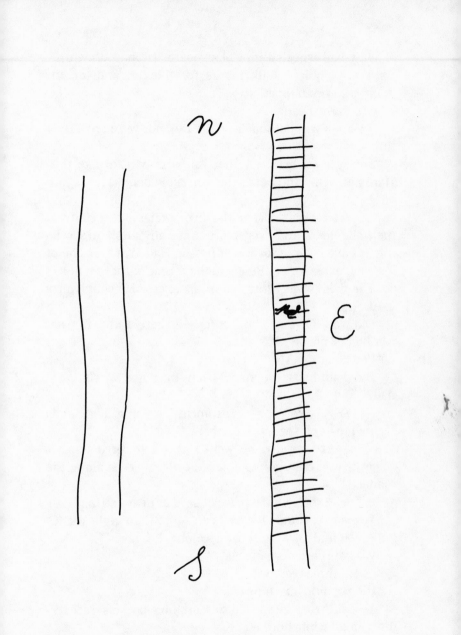

THE MECHANIC'S SKETCH

They had wheeled in a blackboard. He had drawn the track with quick chalk marks for the ties and, at one point, a sort of puppet.

"That's the head."

Her torso was not touching the rail, nor were any of her limbs.

"She was on her back, her knees drawn up like this. Here's an arm. And here's the other, the one that was torn off."

Maigret took a look at the five soldiers, especially at their shoulders and even more especially at Ward's, who might have been in love with Bessie. Had Ward, or one of his pals, made love to Bessie in the course of that night?

"The body was dragged a distance of about thirty yards."

"Did you have a chance to see, before the impact, whether or not she was alive?"

"I couldn't say, sir."

"Did you have the impression that her wrists were tied?"

"No, sir. As you can see from my drawing, her hands seemed to be clasped over her belly."

Then, very rapidly, he went on in a lowered tone of voice, "I was the one who picked up the pieces along the roadbed."

"Is it true you found a piece of cord or heavy string?"

"Yes, sir. It couldn't have been more than eight inches long. You find all sorts of things along the tracks."

"Was the cord near the body?"

"About three feet away."

"Did you find anything else?"

"Yes, sir." And he started to search his pockets, recovering a small white button.

"Looks like a button off a shirt. I put it in my pocket automatically."

He held it out to the coroner, who passed it to the prosecuting attorney, who, in turn, gave it to O'Rourke, whose task it was to show it to the jurors, finally placing it on the table in front of him.

"How was Bessie dressed?"

"She had on a beige dress."

"With white buttons?"

"No, sir. The buttons were beige, too."

"How many trainmen manned your train?"

"Five in all."

Harold Mitchell, Bessie's brother, had once more gotten to his feet. He received permission to speak.

"I ask to hear the four others."

It was the second engineer who said he had seen, or claimed he had seen before the impact, that Bessie's wrists were tied.

"Adjourned!"

Yet something had gone on that Maigret had not completely understood. At a certain point, the prosecuting attorney had gone over and spoken to the coroner, but Maigret had caught only a few words of what he had said. The coroner, in his turn, had made some sort of statement.

Now, at the moment when everyone left the courtroom, the five Air Force men had been led to the end of the corridor by the deputy sheriff with the big revolver, instead of following their commanding officer back to the base as they had done the day before.

Maigret was curious enough to want to go see for himself. There was a heavy iron door, a grille and, behind that grille, other grilles, those of the cells of the prison.

"So they've been arrested?"

At first, the man did not understand him because of his accent.

"Yes, for having contributed to the delinquency of a minor."

"The Chinese too?"

"He paid for one of the bottles."

They were in jail because they had made Bessie drink, Bessie who, at seventeen, had been married, divorced, and had given herself over more or less specifically to prostitution.

Maigret was certainly not blind to the fact that a man on his travels is always a mite ridiculous since he would prefer that things go on as they do at home.

Perhaps they had their own way of doing things. Perhaps this coroner's inquest was only a formality and the true investigation was going on in some other place.

He had proof that same evening. As one of the bar's customers got up rather heavily to leave after calling out a good night to the roomful of clients, Maigret spotted O'Rourke, who had been concealed from him by the drinker.

O'Rourke was seated in one of the booths with a bottle of beer in front of him. The waitress had joined him and sat now beside him. They seemed good friends. The chief deputy sheriff caressed her arm as he spoke to the girl and had offered her a drink.

Did he know Maigret by sight? Had Harry Cole pointed him out among the spectators at the inquest?

Maigret was pleased to see his American colleague at the bar. Wasn't this what he would have been doing in a like situation? This was undoubtedly not O'Rourke's first visit to the Penguin.

He didn't play the cop. He was comfortably seated in

72

his corner, and he smoked cigarettes rather than a pipe. Besides, he made a surprising enough gesture at a certain moment. He lit a cigarette and, after having pulled on it a couple of times, passed it casually to the girl, who put it between her lips.

Had she been here the night Bessie died? Probably. She must be here most evenings. Had she waited on them?

O'Rourke was making a joke and she was laughing. She had served a couple who had recently come in and now had returned to sit beside him.

He acted as if he were making up to her. He was red-haired with a crew cut, and his coloring was reddish, too.

Why didn't Maigret go sit with them? He had only to introduce himself.

Instead, he heard himself say, *"Un demi."* He caught it at once. "A beer!" he said.

The beer was as strong as it is in England. Many customers scorned a glass and drank right out of the bottle. Next to Maigret there was a cigarette machine like the chocolate-vending machines in the Paris subways.

Didn't it all come out in the end?

He had been talking about recruiting for the armed forces and Harry Cole had told him:

"There are a lot of parolees."

Since Maigret did not understand, Cole had explained:

"Here, when a man is sentenced to two to five years in prison, or even more, this doesn't mean that he has to spend all that time locked up. After a certain time, sometimes after only a few months, if his conduct is satisfactory, he is put on parole. He is free, but he must report on his activities, at first every day, then every week, then once a month. He has to report to a police officer."

"Are there many recidivists?"

"I have no current statistics at hand. The FBI complains that we let too many out on parole. There are those who commit a theft or a murder a few hours after they are released. Others prefer to sign up. Sign up for the armed services, that is, which automatically removes them from police surveillance."

"Was this the case with Ward?"

"I don't think so. Mullins, I think, has been taken in several times for minor crimes. Especially beatings and lesser wounds. He comes from Michigan. They're tough customers there."

Another fact that disoriented Maigret was that the individual was almost never from the part of the country where one found him. Here, in Tucson, the coroner who was also the justice of the peace came from Maryland, but had attended a university in California. The engineer who had been on the stand a short time ago came from Tennessee. At the Penguin, the bartender came in a beeline from Brooklyn.

And back there, in the great cities of the North, there were slums, whole poor sections of the city, with houses like barracks, where men led hardened, ethnic-centered lives and where children formed street gangs, neighborhood by neighborhood.

In the South, people outside the cities lived in wooden shacks amid the detritus.

But this was not the explanation, and Maigret knew it. There was something else, and he drank his beer, fixing his colleague and the waitress from afar but with a determined eye.

At a certain point, he asked himself if O'Rourke was not here to keep an eye on *him*. This was not an impossibility. Harry Cole was quite capable—despite his air of playing with life and with people—of guessing that he might come this evening to the Penguin. Perhaps they did not want him poking his nose into this business.

He was wrong to drink too much. Yet what else was he to do? He couldn't sit for an hour in front of a single glass of beer as he would have done at a terrace café. Nor could he wander about alone on foot along the interminable streets. He had no wish to sit through a film or to shut himself up quite yet in his hotel room.

He did as the others. When his glass was empty, he made a sign to the bartender, who filled it up again. He told himself that, on the following morning, he would repair to the drugstore's blue bottle and feel right as rain.

He had jotted down the number of the house where Bessie had lived with Erna Bolton. At last, he slid off the barstool and ambled off in that direction, trying to make out the names, or more often the numbers, of the streets he passed.

As soon as one left the downtown commercial blocks with their brightly lit store windows, the streets were dark, the houses separated from one another by lawns.

Did people decide on purpose not to close their shutters or their curtains?

All the houses had a front porch, and one could see, on almost all of them, families sitting in semidarkness moving gently back and forth in their rocking chairs.

In lighted rooms, more intimate life was to be glimpsed: a couple eating, a woman combing her hair, men reading their newspapers, and from all these houses murmurs of radios filtered out to the streets.

The one in which Bessie had lived with Erna Bolton was a corner house, a ranch type. The light was on. The house looked stylish, almost luxurious. Harold Mitchell and the musician were seated on a couch, smoking their cigarettes, and Erna, in a housecoat, was serving them ice cream.

Maggie Wallach was not there. Perhaps she too worked at a drive-in, serving hot dogs and spaghetti to the occupants of the cars that drew up.

It was all without mystery. Everyone seemed to live with the lights on bright. There were no worrisome shadows skirting the houses, no curtains drawn to shield shuttered interiors. Nothing but these cars going God alone knew where, never using their horns, stopping short at the crosswalks as soon as the lights changed from green to red, and shooting off smartly at the next color change for wherever they had to go.

Maigret did not eat dinner that night. When he got back to the center of town, the drugstores where he had counted on getting at least a sandwich were closed. Everything was closed except for the three movie houses and the bars.

A little shamefacedly, he slunk into one of the bars and then another. He greeted the bartenders familiarly, as he had seen others do, and hitched himself up on a stool.

Everywhere, the same deafening music reigned supreme. Along all the counters, chrome-plated slots linked to the jukeboxes took the patrons' coins. A dial could be turned to make a choice.

Was this, perhaps, the explanation?

He was alone, and he was doing whatever a man who is alone can do.

When he got back to his hotel, he felt terribly heavy, bitter. He went to the elevator but retraced his steps to put Cole's car key in his box. His colleague might need his key early the next morning.

"Good night, sir!"

"Good night."

There was a Gideon Bible beside his bed. In hundreds of thousands of hotel rooms, these bibles in their black leatherette covers had been placed for travelers.

That was it: the bars or the Bible!

Class was being held this morning on the upper floor, and before Ezekiel called everyone to order, people walked up and down on the balcony in the already burning morning sun.

Everyone wore a fresh light shirt, and a shower (plus the blue bottle, no doubt) had dispelled the cobwebs of the night before.

Thus everyone began the day anew, smiling.

Maigret was a little surprised when, on entering the courtroom, he saw that the five stout fellows were no longer wearing their Air Force uniforms but were dressed all in blue. They had on very loose-fitting coveralls, rather like pajamas, which left the neck entirely exposed.

All of a sudden, they no longer looked like such good boys. It was now easier to notice certain irregularities of feature, certain asymmetric details that led to anxious speculation.

The blackboard was once more in place and one noted again the space between the double lines of the highway and those of the track. The chalk marks were once more to be called into service.

"Elias Hansen, of the Southern Pacific."

This was not one of the trainmen Mitchell had asked to be let testify. The witness explained calmly, in a strong, deliberate voice, what his job was. It was he who investigated on behalf of the railroad each time a theft was committed on one of its trains or whenever an accident or violent death took place.

77

He was certainly of Scandinavian origin. His competence was palpable. He was thoroughly familiar with coroners' inquests and addressed himself of his own accord to the members of the jury, as if he were a schoolmaster explaining a difficult problem.

"I live in Nogales. I was alerted by phone a little before six in the morning, and I got to the site in my car by six twenty-eight."

"Were there any other cars near the site when you got there?"

"The ambulance was still there, along with four or five other cars, some of them police cars, the others just those of people who had stopped out of curiosity. A deputy sheriff was keeping people away from the tracks."

"Was the train still there?"

"No. I ran into Sheriff Atwater, who had arrived a little before I did." And he pointed out, among the spectators, someone whom Maigret had noticed before but had not taken as a colleague.

"What did you do then?" Hansen was asked.

The witness got up, went to the board with assurance, and picked up a piece of chalk.

"May I erase?"

Receiving a nod, he then drew his own version of the highway, the tracks, the four compass points, and the directions of Nogales and Tucson.

"First of all, Atwater pointed out tire marks on the highway that showed where a car had slammed on the brakes abruptly before proceeding to park on the shoulder of the road. As you know, the shoulder is sandy. Very clear footprints went from the car."

"Footprints of how many persons?"

"Two, a man and a woman."

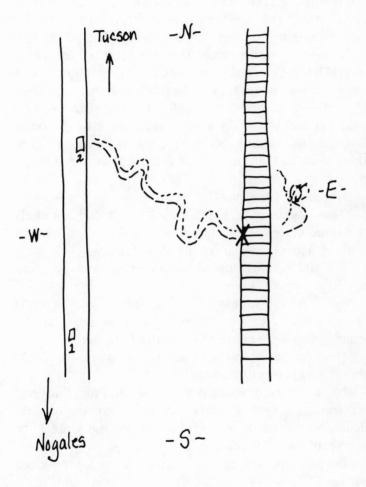

HANSEN'S SKETCH

"Can you trace on the board the approximate route of those footprints?"

He did so in dotted lines.

"The man and the woman seemed to be walking side by side, without following any straight line. They made several detours before they reached the railroad tracks and they stopped at least twice. Then they climbed the siding at this point I've marked with an X. On the other side, a certain distance away, I lost the prints because the terrain is hard and covered with pebbles. We found them again near the spot where the woman was struck by the train. Right on the railbed, which is made up of stone chips, there were no footprints, but a few yards away we found those of the woman."

"Not those of the man?"

"Those of the man, too, but they didn't stop at exactly the same place. At this point, one of them had relieved himself. Traces were clearly visible in the sand."

"Did you notice if any of the footprints were superimposed on others?"

"Yes, sir. Here, and again here, at least twice, the prints of the man's feet were superimposed on those of the woman's, as if the man had come up behind her."

"Have you found footprints of the man on his way back, that is, on his way toward the highway?"

"Not in any continuous, precise fashion. From this point on, footprints become numerous and confusing due, no doubt, to the presence of the trainmen, the ambulance attendants, and the police."

"Do you have the piece of string, or cord, mentioned earlier?"

He pulled it out of his pocket calmly. It was like any old piece of twine and he obviously did not attach much importance to it.

"Here it is. I found another piece just like it about fifty yards away."

"Any questions, Attorney?"

"Yes. How many people were at the site when you arrived?"

"Maybe a dozen."

"Had other people begun their investigations?"

"Deputy Sheriff Atwater and, I think, Mr. O'Rourke."

"You found no further evidence?"

"I found a woman's white leather handbag four or five yards from the track."

"On the side of the footprints?"

"No, on the opposite side. It was partly buried in the soft ground, as if it had been thrown there violently at the moment of impact. We're quite familiar with that. It's the result of centrifugal force."

"Did you open the handbag?"

"I gave it to Sheriff O'Rourke."

"Did your investigation stop there?"

"No, sir. I examined the road, going both toward Tucson and toward Nogales for about half a mile in either direction. At about a hundred and fifty yards in the direction of Nogales, I picked up the tracks of a car that very clearly had stopped on the right shoulder. There were lots of footprints in the sand and on the road, indicating that the car made a U-turn at that point."

"Are the tire marks the same as those of the first car you talked about?"

"No, sir."

"How can you be sure?"

Hansen pulled out of his pocket and enumerated the traces on paper of tire marks from the car that had made the U-turn. Then he showed the others. The four tires of the former car were worn and were clearly of another make.

"Do you know what car these belong to?"

"I checked them out afterwards. They are the tires on Sergeant Ward's car."

"And what about those of the car from which the man's and woman's footsteps lead?"

"I don't think the Sheriff will have any trouble identifying the car. These tires are sold only on credit, on time payments."

"Did you also check out the taxi in which Corporals Van Fleet and Wo Lee, together with Sergeant O'Neil, returned to the site?"

"Yes, sir, I did. That is not the car in question. The taxi is equipped with Goodrich tires."

"Any questions, gentlemen of the jury?"

An adjournment. Maigret lit his pipe and Ezekiel, who did the same, sent him a wink of complicity. The deputy sheriff who carried the big revolver and wore the belt loaded with cartridges led the five fellows in prisoner's garb off down the balcony, and each in turn entered the men's room. Maigret found himself there at the same time as Ward and Mitchell.

Was he mistaken? It had seemed to him that as he pushed the door open Sergeant Ward and Bessie's brother abruptly stopped talking.

5

The Driver's
Deposition

It was on the ground floor during the adjournment that
Maigret found himself alone in a corner of the corridor
with Mitchell, not far from the big red box in which the
Coca-Cola was stored.

Maigret felt as awkward and ill at ease as a country
bumpkin accosting a pretty woman on the streets of Paris.
First, he cast furtive glances around, then he coughed,
trying to look as normal as possible.

"Do you have a photograph of your sister with you?"

A few seconds passed, during whch a phenomenon took
place with which the Superintendent was thoroughly familiar. He had already noted that Mitchell was not of a
particularly pliant mien. Instantly, his features took on
all the hard overtones which made Maigret think of the
tough kids of Paris, rather than of the gangsters in American films. It was an animal defense that such people have
kept; one sees its counterpart in wild beasts who, alone,
suddenly stop dead in their tracks, entirely alert, ears
pricked forward, hair standing straight up on end.

A heavy, immobile look was turned on Maigret, who made every effort to continue appearing relaxed and natural.

Rather gently, to soften the reaction of his interlocutor, he added:

"There are so many questions *they* don't seem to wish to ask."

Mitchell, still suspicious, seemed to be trying to understand him.

"One would say they almost wished it to look like an accident."

"They do wish it."

"You know, I'm in this trade. I'm part of the French police force. This trial interests me for personal reasons. That's why I would like to have seen a photograph of your sister."

Tough kids abound everywhere and are everywhere the same, with the single difference that this one was more bitter than most.

"So you don't believe what these sons of bitches are trying to make you think, that she went and stretched out on the railroad tracks so that the train could run over her?"

Maigret could feel the young man heavy with rage. Finally, he put the bottle of Coca-Cola down on the floor and took a big wallet out of his inner pocket.

"Here she is, three years ago."

The photograph was not a very good one, taken at a county fair, with the girl posed in front of a painted backdrop. The three people in the photograph looked pale and dull. These were certainly not persons from the Southwest, since they were dressed in heavy winter clothes and Bessie had a cheap little furpiece around the collar of her coat with a strange little hat on her head. She looked to be about fifteen, but the Chief Inspector knew that she could not have had those clothes on at that age. The little crumpled face, which did not look like that of a healthy girl, was not without its charm. One felt that she was playing at being a grown-up woman, a woman very proud of going out with two men.

They must have been on top of the world that evening. Certainly they looked as if they felt the world was their oyster. Mitchell, in full-blown adolescence, had his hat tilted over his eyes and a cigarette glued to his nether lip. His expression was defiant.

The second fellow was a little bit older, perhaps eighteen or nineteen, solidly built, yet a little flabby.

"Who is that?"

"Steve. He married her a few weeks later."

"What was his occupation?"

"At that time he was working in a garage."

"Where was the picture taken?"

"In Kansas."

"Why did he divorce her?"

"First of all, he took off without anyone even knowing he was leaving, much less why. During the first months he'd send her a little money; the money orders came from St. Louis, then later from Los Angeles. Finally, one day he wrote that he would rather they got a divorce and he sent her the necessary papers."

"Did he give any reason?"

"I think he didn't want to get my sister in trouble. Six months later he was caught with a gang that stole cars. Now he's in San Quentin."

"You've been in jail, too, haven't you?"

"Only in reform school."

In France, it would have been easier for him. Maigret knew them all and would quickly have climbed the wall that separated them. Here, on foreign ground, he moved with a certain amount of hesitation, anxious not to frighten off his companion.

"Do you come from Kansas?"

"Yes."

"Was your family poor?"

"Yeah. We were starving. There were five brothers and sisters not even a year apart. My father was killed in a truck accident when I was only five."

"Was he a truck driver? Then the insurance must have paid for it."

"He worked on his own. He had an old truck and would haul perishables from the country to the city for the various truck gardeners. He was on the road most nights. The truck wasn't even paid for, so you can imagine that he didn't have any insurance."

"What did your mother do?"

At first he said nothing; he shrugged his shoulders, then said:

"Whatever she could. When I was six, I was already selling papers and polishing shoes in the streets."

"Do you think Sergeant Ward killed your sister?"

"I'm sure he did not."

"Was he in love with her?"

Once more Mitchell shrugged his shoulders, but almost imperceptibly.

"It wasn't Ward. He's too afraid for that."

"Do you think he really intended to get a divorce?"

"Even if he didn't, he never would have killed her."

"What about Mullins?"

"Mullins and Ward scarcely left each other the whole time."

He had taken back the photograph and replaced it in

his wallet. Looking Maigret straight in the eye, he asked him:

"Suppose you discovered who killed my sister. What would you do?"

"I'd tell the FBI."

"It's none of their business."

"Then I'd speak to the sheriff or to the prosecuting attorney."

"You'd do better to speak to me."

And, his expression still a little bit far away, a little bit scornful, he took off because Ezekiel could be heard calling from upstairs:

"Gentlemen of the jury!"

There was once more a confabulation between the coroner and the prosecuting attorney. The latter was saying:

"I'd like to listen to the taxi driver as soon as possible; he's been waiting since this morning and he's about to lose a day's work."

It was always a surprise for Maigret to see the witnesses rising from among the seated public, because, most of the time, they corresponded in no way to the image he had had of them. For example, the driver was this thin little fellow with the thick glasses of an intellectual, dressed in light pants and a white shirt, just like everybody else.

At the beginning of the interrogation he stated that he had been a taxi driver only for the past year, but that previously he had been a botany professor at a college in the Midwest.

"On the night of the twenty-seventh to the twenty-eighth of July, you were flagged down opposite the bus stop by three men from the Air Force base."

"Well, I only learned that from the papers, because they were not in uniform."

"Could you recognize them; and if you can, would you point them out?"

Without the slightest hesitation the driver pointed his finger at O'Neil, Van Fleet, and Wo Lee.

"Did you notice how they were dressed?"

"Well, the first one wore blue jeans and a white shirt or, if it wasn't white, very light. The Chinese had a violet shirt on. I didn't notice the color of his pants."

"Were they all drunk?"

"Not any more than anybody else I pick up at three in the morning."

"Do you remember exactly what time it was?"

"We are expected to write down all the trips we take and to make a note of the hour when we pick people up. It was three twenty-two in the morning."

"Where did they tell you to go?"

"They told me to take the road toward Nogales and added that they would tell me where to stop."

"How long did it take you to get to the place where they stopped you?"

"Nineteen minutes."

"Did you hear their conversation while they were in your cab?"

"Yes."

"Who was speaking?"

"Those two, there."

He pointed to Van Fleet and Sergeant O'Neil.

"What were they saying?"

"That there was no reason why their pal had to stay with them and that he'd do better to keep the taxi to go back to the base."

"Did they say why?"

"No."

"Which one had asked you to stop?"

"It was O'Neil."

"Did they leave you right away? Didn't they ask you to wait for them?"

"No. They discussed the question a while longer. They tried to persuade their friend to go back to the city with me."

"Was it already day?"

"Not yet."

"What did their friend tell them?"

"Nothing. He just got out of the car."

"Who paid for the trip?"

"The two of them. O'Neil didn't have quite enough money for the meter, so the other one made up the difference."

"Didn't it seem to you strange that they had you drive out to leave them in the open desert?"

"Yes, a bit."

"Did you meet any car along the way, either going or coming?"

"No."

"Any questions, Attorney?"

"Thank you. I would like to ask Corporal Wo Lee a question."

The young Chinese came forward once more to take his place on the witness stand, and once more they adjusted the height of the microphone.

"You have just heard what the driver has said. Do you know why your friends tried to persuade you to go back to the base with him?"

"No."

"Why did you not mention this yesterday?"

"Frankly, I had not remembered it."

So he too lied. This was the only one who had not been drinking, the only one whose statements had seemed without any false overtones. Now it seemed that he had blandly hidden the fact that they had tried to get rid of him.

"Are there any other details that you might have omitted telling the jury yesterday?"

"I don't think so."

"Yesterday you told us that when you were walking in the desert, hoping to find Bessie, you were all separated. You maintained a certain distance, one from the other, along parallel lines. What was your position?"

"I walked along the main road."

"Didn't you see any cars pass?"

"No, sir."

"Who was the one nearest you?"

"Corporal Van Fleet."

"So Sergeant O'Neil was walking more or less parallel to the tracks?"

"I think he was on the other side."

"Thank you!"

The following witness was an officer of the highway patrol. He was tall and strong, superb looking in his uniform.

It was the prosecuting attorney who had called him and who now questioned him.

"Tell us what you were doing on the twenty-eighth of July between three and four o'clock in the morning."

"I came on duty at three o'clock in Nogales and I moseyed along in the direction of Tucson, not pushing it to the floor. Before I got to Tumacacori, I passed a truck with a license plate X-3233, coming back empty from California. It belonged to a firm in Nogales. I drew into a side road for a few minutes so that I could take a look up and down the highway: that's a regulation with us."

"Where were you at four o'clock in the morning?"

"I was about level with the airport in Tucson."

"Had you passed any other automobiles or trucks?"

"No. When we pass automobiles at night, we usually register the plate numbers mentally. In fact, what we're doing is comparing them with the numbers on stolen cars that have been sent out to us over the radio. After a while you learn to do it automatically in your head."

"Did you see any people walking along the road?"

"No. If I had seen any at that hour, I'd have slowed up even more and would no doubt have asked them if they needed anything."

"Did you hear a train on the tracks?"

"No, sir."

"Thank you."

So, in spite of what Ward had claimed, his Chevrolet had not been drawn up at the side of the road at that time with the two fellows sleeping inside it.

"Corporal Van Fleet, if you please."

The attorney brightened up, as if he suddenly understood the direction the questions were taking. Meanwhile, O'Rourke continued to lean over him and talk low in his ear.

Perhaps Maigret had been wrong and they still intended to push their inquiry right straight through to the end—but according to certain formulas that were unfamiliar to him.

"You maintain that, when your pal's car arrived there the first time and stopped, Sergeant Ward and Bessie drew away from the car together?"

"Yes, sir."

Pinky was even less at ease than he had been on the previous day. Still, he gave the impression of making a great effort to stick to the things he had said under oath and to tell the whole truth; he kept to his habit of stopping for a moment to think after each question.

91

"Then what happened?"

"The car made a U-turn and Bessie said she wanted to talk to Ward privately."

"That's when you stopped a second time. Look at the blackboard. Is that about the spot, the one marked by an X, that the second stop took place?"

"Yeah. I guess that's about it. I think so."

"You didn't leave the car, nor did your pals, except for Ward and Bessie?"

"That's right."

"And then Ward came back alone. After how long did that happen?"

"After about ten minutes."

"That's when he said: 'Let her go to hell. That'll teach her.'"

"Yes, sir."

"Why did you and O'Neil later on try to get rid of Wo Lee?"

"We didn't try to get rid of him."

"Wasn't there some question of sending him back to town in a taxi?"

"Well, he hadn't been drinking."

"I don't understand. Try to express your thought. Is it because he hadn't been drinking that you wanted him to go back to the base?"

"He doesn't drink, and he doesn't smoke. He's young."

"Go on!"

"It seems that we tried to save him from getting into trouble."

"What do you mean by that? At that moment, did you foresee that you would get into trouble?"

"I don't know."

"When you were walking along looking for Bessie, did you call out her name?"

"I don't think so."

"Was that because you thought she was no longer in a condition to hear you?"

At this, the young Dutchman sat stark still, very red in the face, staring fixedly ahead and quite unable to answer.

After a moment, "Were you able to keep an eye on O'Neil during all this time?"

"He was nearer the tracks."

"I asked you if you were able to see him all this time."

"Not all the time."

"Were there long periods when you would lose sight of him?"

"Fairly long periods. It depended on the lay of the land."

"Could you have heard him?"

"If he had called out, yes."

"But you couldn't hear his footsteps, right? You did not know if he had stopped or not? Did it occur to you to draw nearer the tracks?"

"I think so. We weren't necessarily walking straight ahead of us. We had to go around bushes, cactuses."

"What about Corporal Wo Lee? Did he draw nearer the tracks, too?"

"I didn't see him do so."

"Which of you had decided to make the U-turn when you were all walking toward Nogales?"

"O'Neil remarked that Bessie was certainly not able to go any further. We told Wo Lee to walk along the edge of the highway."

"And then you separated, you and O'Neil?"

"Yes. A little farther out in the desert."

"While you were still with O'Neil, after you had left Wo Lee, did you mention Bessie?"

"No, we didn't say anything."

"Were you still drunk?"

"Probably less so."

"Could you show me on the blackboard the spot where you made this particular stop?"

"I don't know exactly. That's about right."

"Thank you. Sergeant O'Neil, please."

Two or three times, Maigret had felt himself spied upon. It was Mitchell who was keeping an eye on him to note his reactions.

"Do you want to change anything about the testimony you gave yesterday?"

"No, sir."

Was this one, too, born to poverty? He certainly didn't seem that way. He seemed, instead, to have passed his childhood on some farm in the Midwest with hard-working, Puritan parents. In school, he must have been at the top of the class.

"What was the reason you tried to get rid of Wo Lee?"

"I didn't try to get rid of Wo Lee. I thought he was tired and that he'd better get back to the base. He isn't a very strong fellow."

"Was it you who asked him to walk along the highway?"

"I really don't remember."

"While you walked along the railroad tracks looking for Bessie, did you call out her name aloud?"

"I don't remember."

"Did you stop to . . . take a leak?"

"I think so."

"On the tracks?"

"I don't know, exactly."

"Thank you. Coroner, we would perhaps be well advised to listen to Erna Bolton and Maggie Wallach so that we can let them go; they've been here since yesterday morning."

Mitchell's companion was neither pretty nor ugly. She was low-slung in the rear, and her features were heavy. Under the circumstances, since she was going to court, she had put on a dark silk dress and wore stockings and costume jewelry. One could see that she wanted to make a good impression and that she had turned herself out as well as she could.

When she was asked what her profession was, she answered in a very low voice, "I'm not working at the moment."

She tried hard not to look at O'Rourke, whom she seemed to know well. Perhaps at some time in the past she had had something to do with him.

"Did you share your house with Bessie Mitchell?"

"Yes, sir."

"Did Sergeant Ward come several times to see her? And were you present?"

"Not every time."

"Did you ever witness any spats or fights between them?"

"Yes, sir."

"What were they caused by?"

Now that the prosecuting attorney was really into it, the coroner had resumed playing with his adjustable chair; or sometimes he stared at the ceiling, sucking on the end of his pencil. It was extremely hot in spite of the air conditioning. Ezekiel got up to go close the blinds, which at least cut the sunlight into thin slivers. Maigret, seated near the Negress with the baby, still accompanied by her entire tribe, smelled her spicy fragrance.

The pupils of Mitchell's eyes, fixed on his companion who was now seated in the witness box, did not move any more than those of a basilisk.

"Ward always yelled at Bessie that she flirted."

"Flirted with whom?"

"With everybody."

"With Sergeant Mullins, for example?"

"I don't know. I never saw him come to the house. He was there for the first time on the twenty-seventh of July when I met him at the Penguin Bar."

"On the twenty-fourth or -fifth, didn't they have a worse fight than usual?"

"The twenty-fourth. I was just about to go out. I heard . . ."

"Tell us the exact words you heard."

"The Sergeant was yelling, 'One of these days, I'll kill you! That would be the best thing for everybody!'"

"Was he drunk?"

"He had been drinking, but I don't think he was drunk."

"Didn't you talk to Bessie privately during the evening of July 27?"

"Yes, sir. At a certain moment, I pulled her aside and told her, 'You ought to watch out for that guy!'"

"What was that all about?"

"I was referring to Mullins. I added, 'Bill's furious. . . . If you keep it up, they'll have a fight. . . .'"

"If she kept what up?"

"Kept on talking to Mullins."

Perhaps the word talking was something of an understatement.

"Who suggested you continue the party at the musician's?"

"*He* did, Tony, the musician. He said everybody could go over to his place. I think it was Bessie who asked him."

"Was she drunk?"

"Not very. Just about as usual."

"Any other questions?"

Now it was Maggie Wallach's turn. She looked like a

big talking doll with a round baby face and prominent eyes. Her skin was very white and she did not seem to be in good health. Was she the musician's mistress? This was not clear except to Erna Bolton and Mitchell.

"Where did you first meet Bessie Mitchell?"

"We worked at the same drive-in on the corner of Fifth Avenue."

"How long had you been there?"

"About two months."

This girl certainly came from one of the slums of a large city and as a child must have sat out on many a stoop in the midst of noisy, pitiless surroundings.

"Were you present when she met Sergeant Ward?"

"Yes, sir. It was around midnight, a little later, and he came in his car and asked for hot dogs."

"Whom was he with?"

"I think it was Sergeant Mullins who was with him. They talked for a long time. Bessie came and asked me if I wanted to meet them later and I told her that I wasn't free. When they left, she wanted me to tell her what I thought of Ward and told me that he was coming back alone to pick her up later."

"Did he come back?"

"Yes. Just before closing. They left together."

"During the night of the twenty-seventh of July, at the musician's, did you see Ward first enter the kitchen and then hit Bessie?"

"No, sir. He didn't hit her. I was behind him when he went into the kitchen. Bessie was drinking, and he grabbed the bottle out of her hands, almost threw it on the floor, got hold of himself, and put it back on the table."

"Was he furious?"

"Well, he certainly wasn't calm. He didn't like to see her drink."

97

"Yet he had taken her to the Penguin Bar?"

"Yes, sir."

"Why?"

"Probably because he couldn't take her anywhere else."

"At the moment you speak of, did Ward quarrel with Mullins? I am still talking about the scene that took place in the kitchen."

"Yeah, I understand. No, he didn't say anything to him. He gave him a tough look, but he didn't say a word."

"Let's have the next witness!"

They seemed to want to wind up the case that day, and the coroner was less generous with his adjournments.

Tony Lacour, the musician, was thin and scrawny, and his face looked as if he were always in tears or just on the verge of tears.

"What were you doing the night of the twenty-seventh of July?"

"I spent the evening in the Penguin Bar with *them*."

"You weren't working?"

"I'm not at the moment. A couple of days ago, well, ten days ago, I finished my gig at the Puerto Rico Club."

At the moment Maigret was asking himself what instrument he played, the question was asked by the prosecuting attorney, who must have been curious, too. He played the accordion. Maigret would have guessed as much.

"When a row broke out at the Penguin between Ward and Mitchell, did you follow them outside? Do you know what they were quarreling about?"

"I know it had to do with money."

"Didn't Mitchell accuse Ward of having relations with his sister, when he was a married man?"

"Not in front of me, sir. Later, in my apartment, about

the time they had that incident with the bottle, he said Bessie had a tendency to drink and that that was too bad, that she was only seventeen years old and that in bars she always passed herself off as twenty-three; otherwise, they wouldn't have served her."

"Was it you who suggested to the group that they go to your house?"

"Bessie admitted that she didn't want to go home right away and the others said they were going to buy some bottles."

"Did you give Sergeant Ward cigarettes?"

"I don't think so."

"Did you see anybody slip a pack of cigarettes into his pocket?"

"No, sir."

"Did anyone, to your knowledge, smoke marijuana?"

"No, sir."

"What time was it when they left your house?"

"About two-thirty."

"What did Harold Mitchell and Erna Bolton do?"

"They stayed for a while."

"Until morning?"

"No. They stayed maybe another hour or hour and a half."

"Did anyone talk about Sergeant Ward and Bessie?"

"We only talked about Bessie. Harold explained that his sister had taken the habit of drinking too much and that this was terrible for her health because she had bad lungs. He added that she had been in a nursing home when she was little."

"Did Mitchell and Erna go away in a car?"

"No, sir. They don't have a car. They left on foot."

"Was it about four in the morning?"

"Oh, at least. It was already beginning to get light."

"Adjourned!"

Maigret once more found the brother's eyes fixed on him, and this time the glance did not entirely fail to move him.

Mitchell's first reaction to him had been an icy suspicion and perhaps some sort of defiance or scorn, rather than any hope that the Frenchman could answer his questions.

He had been watching Maigret all through the interrogation and now seemed to be saying, "Who knows? Perhaps he isn't like the others. After all, he's a foreigner. He's trying to understand."

Certainly his attitude was still far from friendly, but there was not an unbreachable wall between them any longer.

"You hadn't told me that your sister was tubercular," Maigret murmured as they walked, one behind the other, toward the exit.

Harold Mitchell only shrugged his shoulders. Perhaps he too had had it? No, because in that case he would never have been taken into the army. Erna Bolton was waiting for him under the colonnade. She was careful not to take his arm. They did not speak to one another. She simply followed him in a humble, docile way, and her too heavy rear moved a bit like that of a laying hen.

O'Rourke, ever the eager beaver, was heading with the attorney toward the latter's office, while the five men in their prisoners' outfits were waiting for the deputy sheriff to take them back to their cells. About the afternoon session, Maigret wondered: Would it take place upstairs or down? He had not listened to the coroner's last words. The woman on the jury, who now stood near the Coca-

Cola machine, was eating a sandwich; there wasn't any question that she would sit on the bench in the unshaded patio to knit another square while she was waiting for the afternoon session to resume.

"Downstairs," she answered his question.

Henry Cole was waiting for him at the wheel of the car. There was somebody in the back seat who had one of the inevitable white shirts on. The man was smoking a cigarette.

"Hello, Julius! The session isn't through yet? Sit up front with me. We'll go and grab a bite together."

Once the door had closed, he added, as if he were introducing his friend:

"Ernesto Esperanza! He'll have to have lunch with us, because I have nobody to take him back to Phoenix before this evening and I don't like to turn him over to the county sheriff. Are you hungry, Ernesto?"

"Hungry enough, Chief!"

"Well, profit from it. This is the last decent meal in a restaurant you have much chance of having for the next ten or fifteen years."

Then he said, simply, to Maigret: "Well, I finally caught up with him, but not without him causing me a lot of trouble. He tried to drop me with a forty-two. Open the glove compartment. That's where you'll find his toy."

The revolver was there, a big automatic that still smelled of the shell. Mechanically, Maigret opened the weapon and tipped out the two remaining bullets.

"He almost got me. Didn't you, Ernesto?"

"Yes, Chief."

"If I hadn't stooped down just in time and if I hadn't caught him one in the leg, I'd have had it. I've been trying to catch up with him for the past six months, and as far as he's concerned he's done the very best he could to get rid of me. True enough, Ernesto? Your ribs don't hurt anymore, do they?"

"Not too much . . ."

To the people eating in the cafeteria where the group had lamb chops and apple pie, they were no different from any other three midday diners. Only the following day would the photograph of the Mexican appear in all the papers of the area, with a big headline announcing that one of the most important drug traffickers of the region was finally under lock and key.

"What's going to happen to your five little friends from the Air Force?" Harry Cole asked, wiping his mouth with a paper napkin. "Did they find out yet who the dirty rat is who left little Bessie on the railroad tracks?"

Maigret didn't even wince. This morning he was not in a bad humor.

6

The Buddies
Line Up

Things were growing cozy. In the morning, and especially
after the midday meal, which some ate in the courthouse
patio and others in the square outside, people recognized
each other with pleasure. They exchanged greetings or
made small gestures. By now, everyone knew what seats
the usual spectators would occupy, and even the five Air
Force men no longer looked at members of the public as if
they were intruders.

The coziness was all the more palpable downstairs,
where the members of the jury sat on benches usually
reserved for the public. There they were, side by side with
the curious onlookers. If need be, extra chairs were
brought in. Inevitably, the coroner would scowl at the
great, noisy fan. The water fountain, with its ever-ready
ice water and its cylinder of paper cups, was near Maigret,
so that anyone at a given moment might find himself at
his side.

Ever since he had patted the young black woman's
baby, she had kept his seat for him, and she turned radi-
ant, pearly smiles his way.

As for Ezekiel, he waited for each session to begin before he pounced on whatever new offender dared appear with a cigar or a cigarette. He was a make-believe tough customer with the soul of a playful urchin.

He would rise up all of a sudden, his mustache trembling, his avenging arm outstretched, and cry without regard for whatever the prosecutors might be saying:

"Hey! You, there!"

The whole room would burst out laughing. People would turn around to see who had been caught.

"Put out your cigarette!"

Satisfied, Ezekiel would give a wink visible to the greater part of the room. He had had an even greater triumph the day he had called the prosecuting attorney himself to order. Coming into the room after an adjournment, he had forgotten to snuff out his smoke.

"Hey! Mr. Attorney!"

Maigret could not believe the case would wind up this particular day; he could not believe that, in a few hours, the five men and one woman who made up the jury would be in a position to decide whether or not Bessie's death had been an accident.

If their decision was yes, then the case would be closed, once and for all. If, on the contrary, they decided that the girl's death was due to criminal maneuvers by one or more other persons, then Mike O'Rourke and his men would have all the time they needed to work, pending the final hearing on the case.

It was strange. At breakfast, Maigret had made a little discovery that had amused him, that had given him pleasure especially because it was a sort of tiny triumph over Henry Cole. Cole had not behaved exactly as he had earlier. He had been a little cocky, as if he had been showing off to a pretty woman whom they might have had with them, and Maigret guessed that it was all because of Cole's having taken Ernesto, the drug dealer.

At bottom, Cole felt the involuntary respect, almost admiration, for him that one feels for anyone who has made it to the top of his profession—whether he's a multimillionaire, a screen star, or a famous crook.

The Mexican had brought in over a quarter-million dollars' worth of marijuana in a single drug haul and had had many previous successes. In the hills south of the border, areas accessible only by plane, he owned his own plantations of marijuana.

When all was said and done, if no one expressed great interest in the five members of the Air Force appearing at the coroner's inquest it was because, even if one of them had killed Bessie, he was not a hardened criminal.

Would any one of them have held the police at bay, sawed-off shotgun in hand, forcing them to mobilize all the local constabulary and to use tear gas to reduce the culprit to tractability? Would any one of them have been capable of holding up ten banks, or of wiping out several rich ranchers and their families? In any of those cases, there would have been crowds overflowing the balconies, filling the corridors, and eddying out into the streets.

Didn't this fact explain many things? It was essential to play the game well, no matter what it might lead to.

Mitchell, because he was indeed a tough customer, must be respected in the little circle of persons he frequented, whereas Van Fleet, with his face of a Baby Jesus and his wavy hair, didn't matter. The proof lay in the fact that they had nicknamed him Pinky. Not, as they would have done of a real man, Red, or even Curly!

A deputy sheriff, Phil Atwater, now took his place on

the witness stand. He was the first to reach the scene and the man the inspector for the Southern Pacific had met when he got out of his car.

He did not wear his badge on his shirt. Neither old nor young, he had the sulky expression of those who suffer from poor digestion and who always have someone at home ill.

"I was in the Sheriff's office when, a little before five that morning, we got a telephone alert. I took one of the cars and got to the scene of the accident at about seven past five."

The word "accident" made Maigret wince, and what followed proved he was not mistaken. Atwater, though a police officer, was one of those who hated anything out of the ordinary.

"The ambulance arrived soon after, too, about the same time as I did. The trainmen were the only people along the highway, and there was one car that had stopped a few minutes earlier. I left one of the men I had brought with me on guard, to keep any possible snoopers away from the track. Right away, I found the tire marks of a car that had parked at that point. I surrounded them with a chalk ring and, on the downhill side, the sandy side, with bits of wood stuck into the ground."

Atwater was the very prototype of the conscientious public employee, and he seemed to be defying all the world to find any fault with his performance.

"You paid no attention to the body?"

"Oh, yes! I paid attention to the body, too. I picked up several pieces of flesh and a piece of an arm with the whole hand attached."

He said this in a condescending tone of voice, as if the activity were merely routine. Then he rummaged in his pocket and brought out a little piece of paper.

"Here are a few hairs. They haven't had time to analyze them yet, but at first sight they look like Bessie's hair."

"Where did you pick them up?"

"At about the spot where the impact took place. The body was dragged or rolled some seventy-five feet, I'd say."

"Did you notice any footprints?"

"Yes, sir. I put sticks and bits of wood around them to protect them, too."

"Tell us what sorts of footprints you found."

"Women's footprints. I compared them with one of Bessie's shoes and they matched."

"Were there any masculine footprints near hers?"

"No, sir. At least, not between the highway and the railroad tracks."

"Yet when you followed the company inspector, Mr. Hansen, a little later, he says he saw a man's footprints, too."

"Probably mine."

Atwater did not like to be contradicted and he did not seem to feel any particular fondness for the representative of the Southern Pacific.

"Would you please show us on the board the approximate route of the footprints?"

He looked at the sketch that had been made last and wiped it all off. Then he drew in the track and the highway, and he made an X where the body had been found and another where, he estimated, the impact had taken place.

But he made a mistake in putting "north" where "south" should have been. His sketch had little to do with Hansen's. According to him, Bessie would have made many fewer meanderings and would have stopped only once to change direction.

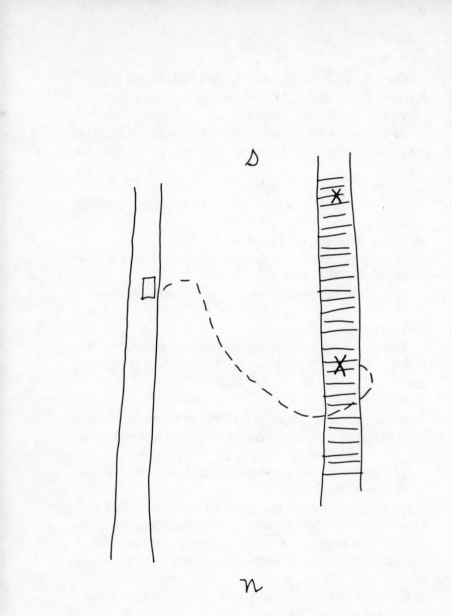

ATWATER'S SKETCH

What did the jury make of these contradictions? They listened and looked with continuous attention, and one felt that they wanted to understand and to do their job conscientiously.

"Is that all you found on this side, I mean to the north of where Bessie died? Did you also look for footprints to the south, that is, in the direction of Nogales?"

Atwater looked at his sketch in silence and, since he had reversed north and south, he took a bit of time to understand what he had been asked.

"No, sir," he said, finally. "I did not consider it useful to look for footprints toward Nogales."

They let him go. He must have had things to attend to at his office, for he left the courtroom immediately, pompous and self-confident.

"Gerald Conley."

He was another deputy sheriff, the one who had so many cartridges in his belt and such an imposing revolver, complete with a sculpted horn handle. He was round all over, and had a high-colored complexion. One could guess that he was a popular figure in Tucson and that popularity in no way displeased him.

"At what time did you arrive on the scene?"

"I was at home, and no one got to me until ten past five. I got to the scene a little after five-thirty, without even stopping long enough to have a cup of coffee."

"Who was at the site?"

"Phil Atwater was there along with the company inspector. Another deputy sheriff was at the scene to maintain order, because a few cars had stopped by then. I found the area marked off with wood stakes and I followed those from one end to the other."

"Were the woman's footprints ever on top of the man's?"

"Yes, sir."

"At about what distance from the road?"

"About forty-five feet from the road. At that point, the prints clearly showed that two people had stopped for a fairly long time, as if they had had an argument."

"After that point, did the prints separate?"

"My impression is that the woman went on alone. She was weaving, didn't walk in a straight line. The masculine footprints found farther on were not those of the same man as the first ones."

Once more, Maïgret began to suffer. He sweated out his impulse to get up and open his mouth to ask specific questions.

It was only natural that the five Air Force fellows contradicted one another. They were like five schoolboys mixed up in a dirty situation, each one of whom wants to do his best to get off scot-free. Besides, they had started to drink at seven-thirty in the evening and were all drunk, except for the Chinese.

But the members of the police force?

One might have thought that the deputy sheriffs were taking this occasion to settle grudges they held against each other. And yet O'Rourke did not bat an eyelid. Seated beside the prosecuting attorney, over whom he continued to lean from time to time to make his comments, he went on smiling serenely.

"Then what did you do?"

"I went south." And one felt his satisfaction at delivering this direct hit at his smug colleague who had just left.

"Someone stopped to relieve himself near the track," he said.

Maigret wanted to ask, "A man or a woman?"

Because, in the last analysis, however trivial it may seem, a man and a woman do not leave the same traces when they pee—the one standing, the other squatting—especially on sandy soil.

The crux of the question lay there, and no one seemed to have noticed it. Nor had anyone asked the doctor if Bessie had made love that night. No one seemed to have examined the underclothing of the five fellows. Instead, they had found it sufficient to ask them the color of the shirts they were wearing.

Given the footprints starting at the car, Ward now ranked first as suspect, provided that, at a certain point, his footprints were uppermost. And provided that his footprints continued as far as the track, as the inspector of the Southern Pacific averred.

Atwater's testimony made Ward's guilt just about impossible—unless the crime had taken place on the second auto trip.

With Conley, the sheriff with the big revolver, everything was once again different. Ward, according to him, could have followed Bessie only some fifteen yards. But then, why did the sergeant claim that he had not followed her at all?

Conley went on:

"It's impossible to pick up the prints either on the road-bed itself, because it is full of pebbles, or in the immediate surroundings, where the terrain is harder than in the desert. But as you walk south and to the right . . ."

"Toward the highway?"

"Yes, sir. Walking at this angle, I was saying, I picked up other footprints."

"Coming from which direction?"

"They came from the highway, farther to the south."

"On a diagonal?"

"No, almost perpendicularly."

"A man's footprints?"

111

"Yes, sir. I planted stakes. The length of the footprint would make me think the man was of medium height."

"Where did this series of prints lead you?"

"To about a hundred and fifty feet from where the car stopped the first time."

Now nothing stood in the way of the fact that Ward had been speaking the truth: that Bessie had gone off with Mullins and had not reappeared.

"Did you pick up any women's prints in this area?"

"No, sir."

So it was not yet settled.

"Are the prints lost once you reach the railroad bed?"

"Yes, sir, they are. One kept on walking at random on terrain where, as I told you, the human footprint leaves no trace."

Adjournment.

O'Rourke passed near Maigret twice on the balcony, and both times he looked at him with a strange smile. There must have been liquor in the office where he withdrew after each session, for when he came out, his breath was strong.

Had Cole told him the identity of this thickset, intensely interested spectator? Was he amused to find him a bit at sea?

"Do you have a light?" the juror with the wooden leg asked Maigret.

"Complicated, isn't it?" Maigret grumbled.

Was he using a wrong word, one that his interlocutor did not understand? Or did the man take literally his instructions not to discuss the case before a verdict was arrived at? Whatever the reason, he responded with a smile and went to station himself in front of the little lawn that whirling jets of water from a hose tried in vain to freshen.

Maigret regretted not having taken notes. At this time it was less the contradictions of the police which interested him than those of the five young men who, at each hearing, seemed to grow farther and farther apart.

"Hans Schmider!"

One could not always determine immediately what a witness was supposed to contribute, and it was a game for Maigret to guess the job or profession of each of them. This one was heavy, or, more exactly, he had a heavy belly that swelled his shirt, like a limp sack, above his too tight belt. His skintight pants did not reach his navel, so he looked as if he had tiny legs and a huge chest.

Schmider's hair was rather long, and stuck out in all directions. His shirt was of dubious freshness. His arms and his chest were hairy.

"You are attached to the sheriff's office?"

"Yes, sir."

His strong and lively voice and almost familiar tone made one realize that he was used to these hearings.

"What time was it when you were called in?"

"About six o'clock. I was asleep."

"Did you go to the site immediately?"

"As soon as I went to the office and picked up my gear."

He was so much at ease, leaning back in his chair, his belly thrust forward, that he automatically put his hand in his pocket and drew out his cigarettes. Ezekiel had just enough time to leap toward him before Schmider remembered where he was.

"Tell us what you saw."

Schmider got up, went to the blackboard, hands in pockets, looked at the sketch on it with a critical eye, and erased it. He had to lean over to pick up a piece of chalk that had fallen to the floor, and his pants were stretched so taut that one expected them to split at any moment.

113

First he marked the compass points, then drew in the track, the highway, then a dotted line that led with many detours from the latter to the former.

Finally, on the edge of the highway, he marked two rectangles.

"Here, at point A, I picked up the tracks of the car we'll call car number one."

He descended from the raised podium long enough to collect a fairly large parcel from the table. He took out a plaster of Paris impression.

"Now here's the tread mark of the left front tire, an old Dunlop."

He himself offered the evidence to one juror after another, as if passing a cake, and he did this later with three other exhibits.

"Did you compare these tracks with those of Ward's car?"

"Yes, sir, and they're the same. There's no doubt about that. Now here are the tracks I picked up from car number two. These are almost new tires, bought on time. The stores that sell tires on credit like that, I had them all cased out. But I don't think we have any results as yet."

So Schmider was the technician in the sheriff's brigade. He was the lab man and had the calm assurance that his occupation implied. It never even occurred to him that any contradiction was possible.

"Did you find any other evidence on the road?"

"By the time I got there, there were several cars, not counting the ambulance and the police cars. I didn't make impressions of any car tracks other than the ones that were pointed out to me and that were particularly clear."

"Who pointed them out to you?"

He turned toward the attorney's table and indicated O'Rourke with one finger.

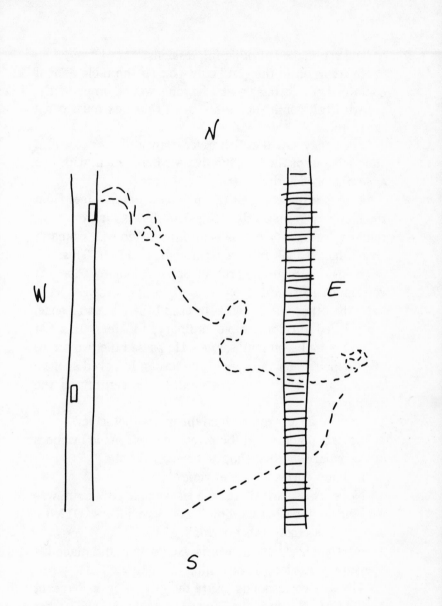

SCHMIDER'S SKETCH

"Did you make any other impressions?"

He returned to the cardboard box on the table as if it contained all secrets, and everyone waited impatiently, yet with full confidence that out of that box must come the truth.

When they saw that Schmider drew a plaster cast of a shoe sole out of the box, the five Air Force men, with one accord, looked at their feet.

"This is an impression taken some forty-five feet from the highway. A man's footprint. The shoe is far from new, the heel, rubber. Now this is an impression of a woman's shoe which I took from a print right beside it. This corresponds exactly to the print of Bessie Mitchell's shoes, as you can easily check."

In the other hand, he fairly brandished a man's shoe, darkish red in color, simple, ordinary, a loafer with a flat heel, that had seen long service. He passed the two pieces of evidence under the eyes of the jurors. It looked as if he would have liked to present them to the scrutiny of the spectators, too.

"Did you do any research on the man's footprints?"

"Yes, sir. I compared the prints to those made by shoes of the deputy sheriffs who had been on the site."

"Did they correspond to anyone?"

"No, sir. Sergeant Ward, as I was able to check out, was wearing high-heeled cowboy boots. Van Fleet's, O'Neil's, and Wo Lee's footprints are smaller."

Everyone hung on his words. He knew it and made his pleasure last as long as he could.

"The size corresponds pretty much to that of Sergeant Mullins, but the shoes he showed me did not have rubber heels."

A sigh could be heard, like a sigh of relief, from out of

the row of Air Force men, but Maigret could not deter-mine which of them had uttered it.

Schmider, who had laid out his plaster casts carefully on the table, now plunged his arm once more into his box and drew out a woman's white leather handbag.

"This is the handbag that was found a few feet from the track, partly buried in the sand."

"Has someone identified this bag?"

"No, sir."

"Sergeant Mitchell!"

Mitchell came forward. Someone held the object out to him and he took it. He opened the bag and took out a coin purse of red silk that contained a few pieces of loose change.

"Is this your sister's handbag?"

"I'm not sure, but I recognize the coin purse that Erna gave her."

From the public benches, the latter spoke up in confirmation.

"It's her bag. We were together when she bought it at a sale a month ago."

There were a few titters. As the trial progressed, people felt more and more relaxed. In fact, they seemed so much at ease that one half expected them to call out to each other, as if they were at the circus.

"Here are a handkerchief, two keys, a lipstick, and a pressed-powder compact."

"Aside from the small change, is there any other money?"

"No, sir."

And Erna interrupted once more, without being called, "I remember she'd forgotten her wallet."

No papers. No identity card. This reminded Maigret of a question he had already asked himself.

A woman's body, badly mauled, had been found on the tracks. Then, a few hours later, before the news had had a chance to get into the papers, the sheriff's men had told Mitchell that his sister was dead.

Who had identified her? How?

He gave O'Rourke a sullen glance. This was the first time he had attended a trial simply as a private citizen, without knowing anything about the background of the case, and he was irritated to feel that many things were consciously kept from him.

But didn't he behave in the same fashion in Paris? In order to feel freer in his work, or to avoid taking an untimely action, did he not withhold some facts he might have known about a case even from the presiding justice?

Was O'Rourke at least going to take advantage of these loopholes?

Did he really want to get at the truth, and, especially, did he want to reveal it?

There were some moments when Maigret doubted it and others when he thought that his colleague, who clearly knew his job, would do what had to be done in good time.

A last piece of evidence was left in the box and Schmider finally brought it forth. It was one more plaster cast, another impression of a footprint.

"This cast was made to the south of the place Bessie died."

In short, it was from the footprints only Gerald Conley had spoken of.

"This here is a size nine, small to medium for a man, I'd say. Corporal Wo Lee wears an eight. Sergeant O'Neil and Corporal Van Fleet wear a nine or nine and a half. The shoes they showed me as having worn at the time don't show the same signs of hard use as these do."

Once more, Maigret had a hard time not getting up to ask permission to question the witness, forgetting that he was not on home ground.

The wall clock over the door that was open and around which curious bystanders lounged, read four-thirty. On the two preceding days, court had been adjourned by five.

Twice already, papers had been brought for the coroner to sign, and he had done his job quietly without interrupting the session.

"Any questions, members of the jury?"

It was the black juror who asked:

"Did the witness pick up the marks of the taxi tires?"

"They were not pointed out to me."

"Does he know anything about the third car? The one that took the three soldiers back to the base?"

"When I got to the site, several cars were already there, and while I was working there several others arrived."

The coroner looked at the clock.

"Members of the jury, we have only to hear from the chief deputy sheriff before you go into consultation. I wonder if it would not be better to stick with it and wrap it up this afternoon."

O'Rourke raised his hand.

"May I be heard? My deposition will not be long, but if it were to be put over until tomorrow morning, you could possibly hear a new witness who could add interesting information."

Maigret breathed easy. In fact he breathed out so loudly, with such an expression of relief, that two of his neighbors turned to look at him. He had been afraid that the case would go to the jury based only on the loose and contradictory testimony heard so far.

It seemed to Maigret unbelievable that the case be closed without further discussion of the third car, the one to which the black juror had just alluded, that had brought the three younger men back to the base and whose whereabouts seemed not to have been found.

Was this the car with the tires bought on time payments? And why had the prosecuting attorney asked not once but twice if the body of the car had been in good condition, or if they had noticed any signs of an accident?

The coroner turned a questioning glance toward the jurors, all of whom, with the exception of the woman, gave quick signs of assent.

Thus, for one day more, they would be *extra*ordinary citizens. As if to confirm the fact, a photographer now crouched down in front of them and a flash bulb went off in the room.

"Tomorrow, then. At nine-thirty. In the second chamber."

Maigret must have been in the photograph since only two people separated him from the foreman of the jury.

He had felt an itch to work with a scrap of paper and a pencil for the past hour. This happened to him rarely, but he wanted to make a point and it seemed to him that in a short time he could manage to eliminate most of the hypotheses.

"They didn't put the other trainmen on the witness stand," a voice near him remarked.

It was Mitchell, sounding ill-tempered.

"The locomotive mechanic who stood on the left in the cab could only see the left side of the tracks, where my sister's legs were. His assistant, who stood on the right, could have seen her upper body. I even asked them to put him on the stand."

"What did they say?"

"They said they'd do it if they thought it was necessary."

"How did they recognize your sister?"

At this, Mitchell looked at him with astonishment and Maigret realized that by asking that simple question, he must have lost prestige in the young man's eyes. He just shrugged his shoulders and let the crowd separate them.

Brusquely he remembered the solitary men sitting in the bars, passing the long evenings gazing at the more or less erotic wall calendars. He remembered, too, the automobiles he had seen parked in shadow, in which one imagined couples holding their breath while he passed.

Harry Cole had not made a date to meet him, but Maigret was sure he would find him any minute now. It was a system that pleased him, Cole's way of saying, "I let you go and come as you please, but you see I always know where to find you."

Just to be contrary, Maigret entered a bar instead of going back to his hotel. The first words he heard were, "Well, hello, Julius!"

Cole was there with Mike O'Rourke seated beside him, nursing a bottle of beer.

"You two know each other? Not yet? This is Chief Superintendent Maigret of the Paris police force, a famous man in his own country. Mike O'Rourke, the most experienced deputy sheriff in Arizona."

Why did he always have the feeling these people were making fun of him?

"A glass of beer, Julius? Mike tells me you've been following the inquest attentively and that you must have your own ideas about the case. I invited him to eat with us. I hope you're agreeable?"

"Delighted."

It wasn't true. He would have appreciated their kind offer on the following day, after he would have had a chance to work out his own ideas. But now he felt as awkward as the two others seemed self-assured, as if they had reached some sort of inner conviction.

"I'm sure," O'Rourke said, wiping his lips, "Chief Maigret must find our methods of questioning witnesses pretty crude, even naïve."

To score a point of his own, Maigret replied, "That waitress in the Penguin Bar, was she able to give you any useful information?"

"Pretty girl, isn't she? She's of Irish descent, like me, and you know the Irish always get on together."

"Was she at the Penguin the night of the twenty-seventh?"

"It was her day off. She knew Bessie very well. And, of course, Erna Bolton and several of the boys."

"Including Mullins?"

"I don't think so. She's never mentioned him to me."

"What about Wo Lee?"

"Never spoke of him, either."

That left Corporal Van Fleet and Sergeant O'Neil. The latter was Irish too, like the chief deputy sheriff.

"Have you found the third car yet?"

"Not yet. I keep hoping we'll find it before tomorrow morning."

"There's a certain number of things I don't understand."

"The number's certainly smaller than it would be for me if I were trying to follow an inquest in Paris!"

"With us, the actual inquiry doesn't take place in public."

O'Rourke gave him an amused glance.

"No more does it here."

"I guessed as much. That doesn't prevent each of your men from saying whatever he wants on the witness stand."

"That's another story entirely. Don't forget that each

one testifies under oath and that in the United States the formal oath is taken very seriously. You can't help but have noticed, too, that they only answer the questions that are put to them!"

"I have noticed especially the questions that have *not* been put to them."

Mike O'Rourke clapped him on the shoulder.

"O.K.! You've got the picture! After we've eaten you can ask me all the questions you want."

"But will you answer them?"

"Probably. So long as I'm not under oath . . ."

7

The Chief
Superintendent's
Questions

It was not Harry Cole but O'Rourke who seemed to be playing host. Instead of taking his guests to a restaurant, he had driven over to a private club toward the center of town.

The public rooms were new, bright, surprisingly modern in design. The bar was probably the most inviting that Maigret had ever seen. While he drank his apéritif, he noticed forty-two separate types of whiskey, not counting seven or eight brandies from France and a bottle of genuine Pernod, which hasn't been seen in any public bar in Paris since 1914.

Facing the bar and highly polished, a series of slot machines listed the usual chances, sporting the tokens of cherries, apricots, plums, and the other fruits laid out in order. When the Inspector wished, almost automatically, to drop a coin in one of these, he noted that instead of the usual modest amount, these machines required fees of a silver dollar or, at the least, a fifty-cent piece.

"I thought such machines were forbidden," Maigret

said. "The day I arrived I read in a Tucson paper that the sheriff had seized a certain number of these machines."

"But that was in public places."

"What about here?"

"Well, we're in a private club."

O'Rourke's eyes were laughing. He seemed only too happy to initiate his colleague into the world of the American West.

"You see, there are many private clubs. You might say that one exists for every social purpose. This one isn't the most elegant, nor is it the most exclusive. There are four or five above this, and then a whole series below it."

Maigret looked about the vast dining room in which they were soon to eat, and he began to understand why restaurants were so infrequent in the big cities.

"Everybody, no matter what type of job he finds himself in, belongs to some club, and his climb on the social ladder is measured by the successive changes in the clubs that he belongs to."

"So that he is free to play slot machines?"

"That's about it!"

With a wink, the sheriff slipped a shiny new silver dollar into the opening of one of the slot machines and scooped up with apparent indifference the four similar coins that spewed forth.

"Downstairs, there's a dice game that corresponds more or less to your roulette. You can also play poker. Don't you have clubs like this in France?"

"We have a few, but they are limited to certain social classes."

"Here there's a club for everybody: there is even one for railway workers and one for post office clerks."

"Then perhaps you'll tell me," Maigret asked, astonished, "why they need all the bars?"

Harry Cole was drinking his double whiskey as if he was performing a rite.

"First of all, bars are neutral ground. You don't always want to meet people in your own category!"

"Just a minute! Stop me if I'm wrong, but don't you mean that one doesn't always wish to *behave* as one must with people in one's own category? I suppose that here, for example, you would not be considered top drawer if you rolled under the table."

"Exactly. If you have to roll under the table, you'd better go to the Penguin Bar or someplace like it."

"I understand."

"There are a few, of course, who don't belong to any category, that is to say, to any club."

"The poor miserable wretches!"

"It isn't only those who don't have any money but rather people who do not want to bow to the customs of certain established social classes. For example, here in Tucson, which has a long history of adjusting to this problem, there is a club in which those of Mexican origin who have become U.S. citizens several generations ago can meet. Now, you're not looked on with favor if you speak Spanish there! Those who still insist on speaking it or who speak English with a heavy accent go to *another* club, one that welcomes newcomers. Have a drink, Superintendent!"

"Tell me, do the soldiers on the base have a club, too?"

"Yes, they have several."

"And must they, too, go to the public bars if they wish to behave in a certain fashion?"

"That's exactly right."

"Our friend Julius is beginning to understand," Cole said, digging hungrily into his meal.

"Many things still seem to me utterly mysterious."

There was wine on the table, a French wine that

O'Rourke had had the sensitivity to order without saying a word. This heavy fellow with the brusque manners did not lack sensitivity. Quite the contrary. And as the evening wore on, Maigret liked him better and better.

"Would you mind if I talked to you about the inquest?"

"That's what I'm here for."

So it had been planned! Perhaps O'Rourke himself had asked Cole to meet his French colleague.

"If I understand correctly, your position here is more or less the equivalent of the one I have in Paris. The sheriff, who is over you, corresponds more or less to the man who, with us, directs the Judiciary Police. Is that right?"

"With the single difference that here the sheriff is elected."

"Now, the attorney is similar to our Public Prosecutor. And the deputy sheriffs you have under your orders are the equivalent of my brigade chiefs and my inspectors."

"I think that's about it."

"I noticed you often cue your prosecuting attorney. And you two probably see to it that unwanted questions are not asked of the witnesses. Am I on the right track?"

"Exactly."

"These witnesses, have you had a chance to question them before?"

"Most of them."

"And did you ask them *every* question?"

"I did the best I could."

"What sort of family does Corporal Van Fleet come from?"

"Pinky? His parents are big-time farmers from the Midwest."

"Why did he sign up for the Air Force?"

"Because his father insisted that he work on the farm with him. He did it very much against his will until two

127

years ago, when one fine day he set out on his own and signed up."

"What about O'Neil?"

"His father is a teacher and so is his mother. These are highly respectable people. They wanted to make an intellectual out of their son, and they found it distressing that he could not get good grades. He, too, was fed up with his situation. Yet while Van Fleet went from the country to the city, O'Neil went from a relatively small city to the country. For almost a year, he worked picking cotton in the South."

"And what about Mullins?"

"He got into trouble very young. He tangled with the police and they sent him to a reform school. His parents had died when he was ten or twelve years old. The aunt who took him in was very rigid and authoritarian."

"When will the doctor's report be complete?"

"I don't quite understand what you mean."

"Five men spent the larger part of a night drinking with a woman. This woman was found dead on the railroad track. But not once during the inquest did anybody bother to mention what had happened between this woman and one or more of the men."

"The question never arose."

"Not even in your office?"

"Oh, in my office, that's different. I can assure you that the autopsy was as complete and careful as an autopsy can be."

"And the results?"

"Yes!"

"With whom?"

It seemed to Maigret that until now he had been dealing with some sort of painted back cloth, like the curtain

128

at the back of a photographer's studio. It was this that they were showing the public, which seemed perfectly willing to accept it.

Now the real characters, with their authentic gestures, actions, and facts, were being substituted little by little for the artificial image.

"Did this take place in the desert? At the musician's?"

That visit to the musician's apartment had been worrying Maigret from the beginning.

"Right off, the doctor discovered that Bessie had had sexual relations with some man in the course of the night but, according to him, it had been quite a while before her death. You know that in these cases one can make a test rather like a blood test and sometimes find out if it was with one or another of a group of men that these relations took place. They spoke to Ward first about it and he turned scarlet. It wasn't out of fright but out of rage, out of jealousy. He leapt up, crying, 'I was damned sure of it.'"

"And Mullins?"

"Yes. He admitted it right away."

"In the kitchen?"

"It was all planned in advance. He had taken Erna Bolton into his confidence, a girl who was furiously jealous of Bessie. For some reason or other, Erna doesn't like Sergeant Ward very much. She promised Mullins, 'Maybe after a while, at the musician's . . .'"

He went on: "She admitted that she acted as lookout near the kitchen. It was she who warned the couple that Ward was coming. And it was to make things look right that Bessie had the presence of mind to grab a bottle of whiskey and pretend to slug down a shot."

Now Maigret began to understand better the attitude of

the witnesses who seemed to pause to think things out before answering the various questions and who seemed to weigh their every word.

"Don't you think these details are relevant for the jury to hear?"

"It's the result that counts, isn't it?"

"And you'll get the same result?"

"I'll see to it."

"Is it out of moral . . . modesty that you omit all sexual questions before the court?"

At the moment he asked this question, Maigret remembered the slot machines in the bar and thought he began to understand.

"I suppose you're trying to avoid giving a bad example?"

"That's about it. In France, if what they tell me is true, you do exactly the opposite. You reveal in the papers every misstep made by any person of importance. For instance, any public figure, any minister. Then when the little man in the street does the same thing, you lock him up. Any other questions, Superintendent?"

"If I had had time, I would have prepared them in writing. Did Erna claim her friend Bessie was in love with Mullins?"

"No. She thought, as I do, that Bessie was truly in love with Ward."

"But she just wanted Mullins?"

"When she had been drinking, she wanted any man who came down the pike."

"Did this happen to her often?"

"Several times a week. But with Ward it was romantic. When he didn't see her, he'd write her, and sometimes he'd telephone her every half hour."

"Did she hope to marry him?"

"Yes."

"What about him?"

"It's hard to say. I'm sure he talked to me sincerely. He's a decent enough guy. He got married, as many of our young people do, after knowing the girl a few days. You meet someone. You think you're in love because you want the girl and you go ask for a marriage license."

"I noticed you hadn't put the wife on the stand."

"What would have been the use? She isn't in good health. She has a hard time bringing up her two children and she's expecting a third. All this is what tethers Ward. He wanted to marry Bessie all right, but he didn't want to make his wife unhappy."

Maigret had not been mistaken when he likened these big fellows to overgrown schoolboys. They played tough. And they thought they were tough. Yet a tough guy from the Bastille area or the Place Pigalle would have put them down as choirboys.

"Was it you, Chief, who identified the body?"

"My men had done it before I got there. Bessie had been to my office five or six times."

"Because she played the prostitute?"

"You always use such explicit terms: that's why it's so hard to answer you. For example, when Bessie worked at the drive-in, she was earning about thirty dollars a week. Now, the house she shared with Erna cost them together only sixty dollars a month."

"Didn't she pick up a little extra on the side?"

"Not necessarily in cash. The fellows would take her out to eat and drink. A cocktail costs half a buck. A whiskey the same."

"Are there many girls like her in the city?"

131

"On different levels. There are those they invite to share spaghetti at a drive-in and those they take out for a good chicken dinner at a restaurant."

"What about Erna Bolton?"

"Mitchell keeps close tabs on her. She would pay a high price if he caught her cheating on him, and I'm sure he'll marry her one of these days. They aren't saints, these boys, but they aren't bad kids, by any means."

"Did Sergeant Mitchell know that his sister and Mullins had had sexual relations in the kitchen?"

"Erna took him to one side to mention it to him."

"What was his reaction?"

O'Rourke started to laugh.

"I wasn't there, Inspector. I can't tell you what no one wants to tell me. Do you know that he was his sister's guardian and that he took his role pretty seriously, at that?"

"You mean by letting her sleep with all the men she wanted?"

"What would you have done in his place? He couldn't be with her from morning till night and from night till morning. He had, after all, to see to it that she earned her living, and she didn't have enough education to work in an office. He tried to get her in as a salesgirl in a local five and ten, but she lasted only a day because she kept getting into conversations with the clients and she couldn't add. As Mitchell saw it, Ward was a sort of last resort. There was a chance that he might end up by marrying her. Mitchell would have preferred Mullins because he was unmarried."

Now it was Maigret's turn to laugh. The appearance of the different characters was changing like lightning as O'Rourke revealed the tales about them.

They had brought brandy, which the chief deputy sheriff was proud to be able to offer his guest because the bottle showed every sign of age. O'Rourke, who must have heard that cognac should be decanted before it is drunk, held his glass religiously in the palm of his large hand.

"To your very good health!"

What surprised Maigret was not the forbearance of men like his colleague or like Harry Cole, who would take his prisoner out for lunch at a good restaurant. This type of forbearance existed in the Paris police force too. There were certain tough characters, well known to the Paris police, whom Maigret understood backwards and forwards. When he would run across them every so often, he would say: "You've been let loose too long, my boy. I'll have to arrest you. It'll do you good to think things over in quiet for a few months."

No, what astonished him was the attitude of the jurors and of the public. When, for example, the witnesses, describing their drinking bout of the night in question, had mentioned the number of rounds, no one had so much as raised an eyebrow.

Every one of these people seemed to understand that it takes all kinds to make a world and that, inevitably, in any society there is a certain quota of total losses.

At the top, there are the big gangsters who are almost indispensable, since, thanks to them, people can get what the law forbids them to have.

The gangsters, in turn, need their killers to see that their orders are carried out.

Not everyone in the world can belong to a club of a predetermined social class. Not everyone in the world can have upward mobility.

There are those who have downward mobility. And then there are those who are born at the bottom. There are weak people, those born under an evil star, and those who turn into bad pennies in order to make themselves believe that they are in some way special.

They needed something to swagger about.

But these quite ordinary people all seemed to understand this.

"Did Van Fleet have a mistress?"

"You mean, did he go to bed with a woman more or less regularly?"

"Have it your way."

"No. It's harder than you think. Aside from a Bessie or an Erna Bolton, a single woman in a situation like this always manages to get herself married. Bessie had almost made it. And Erna will make it."

"So that he could only count on rare occasions?"

"Rare indeed, yes."

"What about O'Neil?"

"O'Neil too. Let me point out to you that Ted O'Neil, despite appearances, is the most timid of the whole batch. He feels out of place. He isn't in his usual atmosphere. He has been brought up strictly enough. Sometimes I think that he misses his family and the more or less established, stable atmosphere from which he is now excluded."

"Don't his parents write to him?"

"They won't have anything to do with him."

"What about Wo Lee?"

"When you have lived in a city in which there are several hundred families, you'll find out that you'd do better not to try to understand them. I think Wo Lee is a good young man and that his ambition is to do the right thing. He is proud of his uniform. He'll get himself killed bravely in the next war."

Harry Cole, who had had almost no part in the conversation, looked at both of them with an enigmatic smile.

"I know a little about the Chinese," he said now.

"What do you think of them?"

"Nothing!" he said ironically.

Most of the people in the club had finished their dinners and more had come into the bar where bursts of voices and clinking glasses could be heard. In a neighboring room people were playing cards.

"Any more questions?"

"Yes. I don't know just how to put this one. I keep coming back to the fact that there were five men and one woman and that they had all been drinking. You told me that Mullins did not resist the temptation. Now, he had had what he wanted. That left three others. Do you believe that a hot-blooded boy like Van Fleet or a solid fellow like O'Neil did not also want Bessie?"

"It's quite possible that they did."

"Don't you think that she could have played the same game with them that she had played with Mullins?"

"It's even probable. She certainly set them on fire, if that's what you mean."

"Do Chinese, like certain blacks, have any particular predilection for white women?"

"Your question, Harry."

"No, I don't think their taste runs in that direction. If they had their way, they would prefer other Chinese. But then, with them, it's always a question of pride."

"So that," Maigret went on, returning to his original idea, "there were five men and one woman in the car. In the back, if I'm not mistaken, in the dark, there were three people, pressed one against the other. O'Neil, Bessie, and Wo Lee. Now wait a minute! I started at the wrong end. You said Ward was jealous. He knew Bessie's temperament and her behavior when she had been drinking. Yet, wasn't it he who organized this night out with his pals?"

"You don't understand."

"I think I do understand but I would like to know if my reasoning works for Americans."

"Well, Ward was proud that he, a married man, had what you would call a mistress. Just imagine how superior he must have felt in relation to his pals."

"But he ran a risk."

"He wasn't thinking of the risk but only of lording it over the others. Notice that at a certain moment he became worried about Bessie's drinking and tried to prevent it."

"He only seems to have been jealous of Mullins."

"He wasn't so far wrong. In his eyes, Mullins was the good-looking guy who attracted women. He didn't pay much attention to the two others, who are almost a head shorter than he. And the Chinese boy bothered him even less, just because he *is* a boy."

"Then you admit to a certain type of exhibitionism."

"I have heard tell that in Paris, as well as in other big cities, the most highfalutin people proudly show off their wives or their mistresses at the opera or wherever, in very low-cut dresses."

"Do you think that something happened in the car that convinced Bessie she didn't want to go to Nogales?"

"There is a sort of explanation, but I don't know whether it will hold water. After he broke into the kitchen, Ward turned nervous and bad-tempered. He forced Bessie to change places and to sit in the back of the car in order to separate her from Mullins. At the same time, this separated her from him. It was like a sulk of some sort. She could very well have answered his sulky state by sulking in turn."

"What if something had frightened her?"

"You mean some gesture on the part of O'Neil or the young Chinese in a car in which there were six people? Don't forget, Inspector, that all these people, with the exception of Wo Lee, were more or less drunk."

"Is that why their depositions don't agree?"

"That, and also, I'll admit, because each one of them feels himself more or less under suspicion. Besides that, these men are friends. O'Neil and Van Fleet are almost inseparable, and you have noticed that their testimony is almost identical. Wo Lee tries to get on with everybody, because he rejects the role of being a stool pigeon."

"Why would Ward have stated that Bessie did not get back in the car after their first stop?"

"Because he's afraid. Don't forget that this incident plunges him into troubles of all kinds right up to his neck. He has a wife and children, and now his wife will probably ask for a divorce."

"He stated that Bessie had gone off with Sergeant Mullins."

"Can we prove the contrary?"

"Your deputy sheriffs contradict each other, too."

"Each witness is under oath and must say what he thinks to be the truth."

"Well, the inspector of the Southern Pacific seemed to me to know his business."

"He's a very solid man."

"What about Conley?"

"A decent fellow."

"Atwater?"

"A total ass."

He did not hesitate to pass strict judgment on his subordinates.

"And what about Schmider?"

137

"He's an expert of the first order."

"Do you really think you'll find the car that brought the three young men back to the base?"

"I'd be very surprised if it's not outside my office tomorrow, because, just this afternoon, we found the address of the garage that sold the four tires on credit."

"Is that why the rest of the inquiry was put over until tomorrow?"

"That, and also because the jurors will be rested and more on their toes."

"Do you think they're on to something?"

"They were very attentive. As things stand now, they probably feel a bit lost. It would be enough tomorrow to bring them a certain amount of hard evidence, if there is any."

"And if there isn't any?"

"Well, they'll make up their minds according to their consciences."

"With such a system, isn't there a risk that a lot of guilty people will go scot-free?"

"Isn't that better than the risk of convicting innocent people?"

"Why did you go back to the Penguin Bar yesterday?"

"I'll tell you. Bessie lived right near there and she went to the Penguin Bar nearly every evening. I wanted to make up a list of the men she must have met habitually."

"Did the waitress give you any interesting information?"

"She told me that Van Fleet and O'Neil came in several times."

"Together with Ward?"

"No."

"Had they ever gone out with Bessie?"

"No. It seems that Bessie didn't like them much."

"Would that exclude the possibility that Bessie had a

date with either one of them? O'Neil could have talked to her in the back seat and asked her to get rid of the others."

"Yes, I'd thought of that."

"She had expressed the intention of not going as far as Nogales, quarreled with Ward on purpose, refused to get back in the car, and waited for the two others in the desert. These two, as soon as they got to Tucson, dropped their friends without even suspecting that Ward and Mullins also intended to return to the site. They tried to get rid of Wo Lee, who was not in on their scheme, and then took a taxi."

"And then they killed her?"

"I think I would have looked over the men's underclothes, both of them."

"That was done. As far as Van Fleet is concerned, the inspection of the underclothes was negative, if I understand what you mean. As far as O'Neil is concerned, it was too late, as his underclothes had already been sent to the laundry when we asked him for them."

"Do you think Bessie was killed?"

"You must understand, Superintendent, that here we believe no one is guilty unless we have the proof of it. Every man is presumed innocent."

Maigret replied, half joking and half serious: "Every Frenchman is presumed guilty. And this, despite the fact that it was you, I'd guess, who picked up the five young men under the charge that they were inciting a minor to drink."

"Well, did they offer her drinks or not? Didn't they admit it?"

"Yes, but . . ."

"They broke the law and that's enough for me because it simplifies my work of getting them all into jail. I don't have too many men at my disposal. If they were merely

139

suspects, I'd have to have all five of them tailed. Well, it seems to me that now you know just as much about this as I do. If you have any other questions to ask me, I'm at your disposal."

"Was it immediately after he learned of his sister's death that Mitchell said she had been killed?"

"That was his first reaction. Don't forget that he knew she had had sex with Mullins in the kitchen and that Ward had almost caught them at it."

"No!"

"What do you mean?"

"Mitchell never suspected Ward. Or at least he had not suspected it at that time."

"Did he tell you this?"

"Well, he gave me to understand as much."

"You know more than I do about this; it sounds like I would be wise to have a conversation with him on the subject. In any case, I must leave you now to go to my office. Harry, you'll stay with the Superintendent, won't you?"

Maigret soon found himself on the street with Cole, whose car was not far off, as usual.

"Where would you like to go, Julius?"

"I'd like to go to bed."

"Don't you think it's the right moment for us to have a nightcap?"

That was it. They had just come from a club where they had every kind of possible drink at their disposal, plus an agreeable atmosphere. Cole knew everyone. There they could have gone on drinking and talking as long as they wished.

Yet, as soon as they hit the street, he wanted to go put his elbows on some anonymous bar. It didn't matter to him too much which.

140

Wasn't there something in this like the attraction of sin?

Maigret almost left his companion to wander back to the hotel, for he really wanted to go to sleep. But through some sort of weakness, he followed meekly, and the latter, quite naturally, stopped the car opposite the Penguin.

It was almost deserted that evening. As usual, it was half dark, and the music droned on from the luminous machine. Surrounding the shiny jukebox were a few tables with couples seated: Harold Mitchell was there with Erna Bolton, and nearby, the musician with Maggie.

Mitchell frowned when he saw the Inspector enter accompanied by the FBI man, and talked behind his hand with his companions.

"Are you married?" Maigret asked Cole.

"And the father of three children. They're off in New England because I'll only be here for a few months."

Suddenly there was a trace of nostalgia in his glance, and he emptied his glass at a single draft.

"What do you think of the club?" he asked, in turn.

"I couldn't have imagined finding a place so luxurious."

"There are even better. At the country club, for example, you'll find golf, several tennis courts, and a magnificent swimming pool."

Cole, who had made a sign to the bartender to refill his glass, went on: "You eat much better, and it costs less than in the restaurants. Everything is top quality. Only you must admit that . . . there isn't an exact word in English. I believe that in French you say it's *emmerdant*."

Strange people, these Americans! They themselves set their own strict rules. Those rules were conscientiously applied and they followed them for so many hours a day, so many days a week, so many weeks of the year.

Did they all feel a need to break out at a certain moment?

It was much later, around closing time, that Cole—who had drunk a great deal and who today was aggressive only toward himself—told Maigret a secret.

"You see, Julius, so that the world can go round, it's essential that people live in a certain way. Here they have comfortable houses, all sorts of electrical appliances, a first-rate car, a well-dressed wife who turns out handsome children and keeps them neat and clean. You belong to your local church and to your club. You earn money, and each year you work in order to earn a little more. Isn't it pretty much that way the world over?"

"Well, perhaps it's more nearly perfected, as a system, in your country."

"That's because we're richer. This is the only place in the world where there are poor people who have their own car. The blacks who pick cotton almost all have an old jalopy. We've cut the losses to a minimum. We're a great people, Julius."

And Maigret replied, not solely from politeness:

"I'm convinced of it."

"Just the same, there are moments when the comfortable house, the smiling wife, the slicked-up kids, the automobile, the club, the office, the bank account all turn out not to be quite enough. Does that ever happen in your country, too?"

"I think it happens to everyone."

"Well then, Julius, I'm going to give you my prescription, which we seem to practice here pretty much by the millions. We go to a bar like this one, and they're pretty much the same anywhere. The barman knows you well enough to call you by your first name; or he'll call you by somebody else's name, say, Joe, if he doesn't know you. It's of little importance. He pushes a glass toward you and fills it with the drink you want whenever it gets empty.

"At a certain moment, someone you don't know taps you on the shoulder and tells you the story of his life. Most the time, he shows you a photograph of his wife and his children and he ends up by admitting that he acts like a pig.

"Sometimes a sad drunk looks at you and, without any obvious reason, takes a crack at you.

"It doesn't matter. The evening ends when you're all put out at one or two or three in the morning because that's the local law, and no matter what happens, the law is still the law.

"You try to get home without upsetting the nerves too much because you risk going to jail if you drive when you're drunk. And the following morning you pick up the little blue bottle which you now know. You let out a couple of belches, a smell of whiskey. You take a good hot bath followed by an ice-cold shower, and the world looks all tidy and new; you feel almost happy to find yourself at home where everything is in order, the streets well cleaned, the car relatively noiseless, and the office air-conditioned. Life can be beautiful, Julius!"

Maigret, meanwhile, was looking at the two couples in the corner near the record player, who were looking at them. In short, it was so that life can be beautiful that Bessie was dead!

8

The Negro
Intervenes

All five of them were there on the balcony of the second floor in their blue prisoners' uniforms. Many washings had turned the cotton of their clothes to that blue one sees in the nets used to catch sardines—the same blue the sky reveals each morning in all its purity.

In a corner in shadow, a little of the cool of the previous night and dawn still lingered. If one moved away from it across the line of sunlight, waves of burning heat scorched the skin.

Later on, when the sun would be even higher in the sky, one of these five men would perhaps be accused of having committed a premeditated murder or at least manslaughter.

Were they thinking of this? And were those of them who knew themselves to be innocent asking whether or not one of them had committed murder? Or did they know which one it was and had they simply kept quiet out of solidarity or friendship?

What struck Maigret was their isolation.

They belonged on the same base and to the same unit. They had gone out together, had had their drinks together, had had their fun together, and all of them called the others by their first names.

Yet from their first appearance before the coroner, invisible partitions had been raised between them and it was as if they had ceased to know each other at all.

More often than not, they tried to avoid looking at each other, and when by chance their eyes met, the expression was sad and heavy, full of suspicion or rancor.

Occasionally, by chance, they touched one another or found themselves elbow to elbow. Yet even touching did not succeed in establishing any real contact between them.

Despite this, certain bonds existed among these men, which Maigret had guessed from the first and which he was now beginning to understand better.

For example, they broke into two distinct groups, not only when they were on leave, but inside the unit as well.

Sergeant Ward and Dan Mullins formed one of these groups. They were the older. One could say they were the grownups; beside them the other three looked like simple blue-clad figures who constituted a younger class.

As if they had been younger pupils with their elders, these three seemed a little awkward and indecisive. One read in their eyes a kind of admiration mingled with envy for those older than they.

But it was between Ward and Mullins that the partitions seemed to have grown thicker, almost impenetrable. Could Ward forget that Mullins had possessed Bessie, taken her almost in front of his eyes in the kitchen of the musician's flat, and that this was no doubt the last embrace she had ever known?

Ward, on the other hand, had paid a high price to possess her: he had promised to divorce, and that meant that he would certainly have had to separate from his children. He had put everything into this game, whereas his friend had had only to look at Bessie as if he were a man about town and she would be his.

Did Ward not have even graver suspicions about Dan Mullins? When he spoke of the drug that had been administered to him, must he not truly have believed that he had actually been drugged?

He had fallen asleep all of a sudden, and his pride as a drinker prevented his admitting that it had been the alcohol. He was not sure of the length of time he had slept. On this point, Maigret made one amusing note: each time the coroner or the attorney had asked precise indications of what time it was, the men had answered:

"I didn't have my watch on."

This had brought to mind his own military service, when soldiers drew not much more than one sou a day; after a few weeks all the watches in the regiment were in hock.

What proved to Ward that Mullins had actually stayed by him in the car?

Maigret had asked Cole, who knew about such things since drug traffic was his specialty: "Couldn't the musician have had marijuana cigarettes at his apartment?"

"First of all, I am almost certain that he didn't have any. And then even if he had had, they would never have plunged Ward into such a heavy sleep as he describes. He would have felt, on the contrary, abnormally vital."

As for Mullins, he must have suspected Ward of having taken advantage of his sleep to reach the railroad tracks.

Yet never once did Maigret observe a glance of hatred or reproach passing between them. One would have said, from their intent look and furrowed brows, that each was

146

trying his utmost to find his own solution to the problem.

In the younger class, Van Fleet was the most nervous of the three. Only that morning, his eyes looked like those of someone who had not slept all night or who had been crying for a long time.

His glance was fixed and anxious. He seemed to foresee imminent misfortune and his fingertips were red, as he had bitten his nails down to the quick. Inadvertently, at times, he still was chewing his fingers; he stopped and tried to pull himself together only if he saw someone noticing him.

O'Neil, pigheaded and sullen, always seemed like the good child who is being unjustly punished for some infraction; he was the only one of the five to wear a prisoner's uniform much too big for him.

The Chinese, in his glance and in his delicate face on which the characteristics were as yet scarcely sketched in, had something in his attitude that was so pure that one still felt like treating him as a child.

"Last day!" a joyous voice whispered in Maigret's ear, making him jump.

It was one of the jurors, the oldest, who looked to him as if he were an old etching. His eyes, encircled with a thousand deep lines, twinkled with malice and yet with good humor. He had seen Maigret so attentive and so assiduous in his attendance, he had felt his passionate interest, and he must believe that he was somewhat disappointed to see the trial end so soon.

"Last day, yes."

Did the old man, who seemed in no way worried, have some idea as to how the case would turn out? Van Fleet, who was the nearest to them and who had certainly heard, began to chew his nails once more, while Sergeant Ward fixed his dark glance on the thickset man with the foreign accent who seemed to be interested in him, God alone knew why.

They were all freshly shaved. Ward had even had his hair cut; they had clipped it closer on the back of the neck and around the ears than usual, so that the very white skin that showed in those areas contrasted strangely with the suntanned skin of the rest of him.

Something unusual was going on. It was already twenty minutes of ten and Ezekiel had not yet called the jurors to order.

He was not outside on the balcony but downstairs in the shade, near the little lawn, smoking his pipe tranquilly in front of a closed door.

Not the coroner nor the attorney nor even O'Rourke, who habitually came and went in the corridors, had put in an appearance yet.

The regulars had gone to take their places in the courtroom as early as nine-thirty, but then they had gone out again one by one, leaving behind their hat or any object recognizably their own in order to keep their place. They looked at Ezekiel from a floor above. A few of them went down to get a Coca-Cola. The Negro woman with the baby turned to talk to Maigret, but he did not understand what she was saying and simply smiled at her, then tickled the chin of the baby with one finger.

He too left the courtroom and saw that there was a meeting in the coroner's office; he recognized O'Rourke, who was on the telephone.

He slipped a coin into the slot of the machine and drank straight from the bottle his first Coca-Cola of the morning. From the street level, he continued to keep an eye on the five men, who were now leaning their elbows on the balustrade of the second floor with their fists propping up their chins.

It was at that point that he took a piece of paper from his briefcase and scratched a few notes on it. Under the archway there was a newspaper vendor who also had a few postcards. He sold envelopes too, and Maigret bought one, slipped his note into it, sealed it, and wrote the name of O'Rourke on it.

Little by little, one could feel impatience coupled with a certain anxiety mounting in the atmosphere. Everyone had ended up gathering outside the door behind which the officers had closeted themselves, and sometimes one saw a deputy sheriff come out, businesslike, about to rush off toward another office.

Finally a light-colored car stopped in front of the colonnade, and a little man with a squat, dumpy body got out and crossed the patio, going toward the sheriff's office. They must have been waiting for him because O'Rourke, rushing to meet him, led him into the office, and the door closed on the two of them.

At five minutes of ten, Ezekiel, having a last pull on his pipe, let out his traditional "Gentlemen of the jury!"

Each one went back and took his place. The coroner tried various positions in his movable chair and adjusted the microphones. Ezekiel, after playing a few seconds with the knobs of the air conditioner, went to close the blinds.

"Angelino Pozzi!"

O'Rourke sought Maigret with his eyes and clearly winked at him. Harold Mitchell, seated a bit farther off, caught the glance and seemed annoyed by it.

"Are you a fruit and vegetable wholesaler and a supplier for the Air Force base?"

"Yes, I supply the officers' mess and the noncoms' mess."

Originally from Italy, Pozzi had not lost his accent. He was obviously very hot. He had hurried and was constantly wiping his face, looking about him with curiosity.

"Do you know anything about the death of Bessie Mitchell, or have you heard about the coroner's inquest?"

"No, sir. I arrived just an hour ago from Los Angeles, where I had gone with one of my trucks to pick up my foodstuffs. My wife told me that several times people had telephoned during the night to ask if I was back yet. Then a little while ago, just as I was about to take a shower and catch some sleep, a man from the sheriff's office turned up."

"What sort of work have you been employed in from July 28 until this morning?"

"As I left the base where I had gone to get my orders . . ."

"Just a minute. Where did you pass the night from the twenty-seventh to the twenty-eighth?"

"In Nogales, on the Mexican side. I had just bought two truckloads of cantaloupes and a truckload of vegetables. We spent part of the night together, my suppliers and I, as we often do."

"Had you been drinking a lot?"

"Not much. We played poker."

"Did anything else happen to you?"

"We went to take a last drink at the private part of the club, and while my car was parked out front, another car must have hit it because I found one fender smashed in."

"Describe your car, please."

"It's a beige Pontiac I bought second-hand only about a week ago."

"Did you know that the tires had been bought on credit?"

"No, I didn't know that. I often buy and resell used cars. Not so much to make a profit as to do somebody a favor."

"About what time was it when you started back toward Tucson?"

"It must have been about three o'clock in the morning when I passed the border. I chatted for a minute with the immigration officer, who knows me very well."

Pozzi had kept the European habit of gesticulating as he spoke, and he looked at the various people who surrounded him one by one as if he did not yet understand what was wanted of him.

"Were you alone in your car?"

"Yes, sir. As I approached the Tucson airport, I saw somebody signaling for me to stop. I decided that he was hitchhiking and I was only sorry that it hadn't happened sooner, because I would have had some company that way."

"About what time was it then?"

"I wasn't traveling very fast. It must have been a little bit after four."

"Was it daylight yet?"

"Not yet, but the night was no longer quite so dark."

"Please turn around and indicate to us which one of these men flagged you down."

Pozzi did not hesitate.

"It was the Chinese."

"Was he alone at the side of the road?"

"Yes, sir."

"How was he dressed?"

"I think he had on a mauve or violet shirt."

"Did you see any other cars before you got to Tucson?"

"Yes, sir. About two miles farther on."

"Headed toward Nogales?"

"Yes, headed toward Nogales. A Chevrolet was stopped on the side of the road right in front of a telegraph pole.

Its lights were out, and for a moment I thought there had been an accident because it was almost touching the pole."

"Did you notice anybody seated inside it?"

"No, it was too dark."

"What did Corporal Wo Lee say to you?"

"He asked me if I would be good enough to wait for his two friends, who would be coming up in a minute or so. He added that all three of them belonged to the base, and I told him that I was just going there. I thought the two others had simply gone off to the side of the road to . . . relieve themselves."

"Did you wait long?"

"It seemed long enough to me, yes."

"About how many minutes did you wait?"

"Perhaps three or four. The corporal called out their names, cupping his hands around his mouth so his voice would carry in the direction of the railroad tracks."

"Could you see the tracks?"

"No, but I take that road often enough to know where the train runs."

"Did Wo Lee move away from the car?"

"No. I saw that he had just about decided to leave without his friends if they did not come along right away."

"Was he inside the car?"

"No, he stayed outside, leaning on the front fender."

"Was this the side that had been hit in Nogales?"

"Yes, sir."

Maigret understood. The police had already found flakes of paint along the road, and that is why they asked the three men if the car in which they had returned to the base bore any traces of an accident.

"Then what happened?"

"Nothing. The two others came up at that point. First we heard their footsteps."

"Did they come from the direction of the tracks?"

"Yes."

"What did they say?"

"Nothing. They just got into the car as soon as they reached it."

"Did they sit in the back seat?"

"One of the two sat behind with the Chinese. The other sat up front beside me."

He turned around and, without having been asked to do so, indicated O'Neil.

"That's the one who was in front."

"Did he talk with you?"

"No. He was very red in the face and his breath was coming in noisy gasps. I decided he was drunk, and that perhaps he had just vomited."

"Did they talk among themselves?"

"No. To tell you the truth, I started to talk to myself."

"From there to the base?"

"Yes. I let them off in the first open area immediately inside the barbed wire. I think the Chinese was the only one who bothered to thank me."

"Did you find anything left in the car by any of them?"

"No, sir. I took care of my business and went back to my house. I frequently spend a night without being able to catch any sleep. The driver came to get me with one of the trucks, and we immediately started out toward Los Angeles. We left there yesterday at noon. I didn't have a chance to read the papers because I was very busy."

"Any questions, gentlemen of the jury?"

Several of these shrugged, and Pozzi, picking up the straw hat that he had placed on the floor, turned toward the exit.

153

"Just a minute. Would you be so good as to remain at the disposal of the court a little bit longer?"

There was no place for Pozzi to sit down, so he stood outlined in the doorway and lit a cigarette, thus drawing down the fulminations of Ezekiel.

At the moment when O'Rourke finally rose to his feet, the old Negro on the jury raised his hand as if he had been in school.

"I would like to ask each of the five men to answer under oath when he saw Bessie Mitchell, alive or dead, for the last time."

Maigret started and looked at the juror with blank astonishment mingled with admiration. O'Rourke, sitting down again, turned toward him and threw him a glance which expressed, "Not so dumb, the old fellow!"

Only the coroner seemed annoyed.

"Sergeant Ward!" he called.

And when the sergeant was seated before the microphone, he said: "You heard the juror's question. Let me remind you that you are speaking under oath. When did you see Bessie for the last time, alive or dead?"

"On July 28 in the afternoon. Mr. O'Rourke took me to the morgue so that I could identify her."

"When did you see her before that for the last time?"

"When she left the car accompanied by Sergeant Mullins."

"That was when you stopped the car for the first time on the right side of the road?"

"Yes, sir."

"When you got out the next time to go search for her, did you even catch a glimpse of her?"

"No, sir."

The Negro juror indicated that he was satisfied.

"Sergeant Mullins! I am about to ask you the same

154

question, and I remind you that you are likewise under oath. When did you see Bessie for the last time?"

"When she got out of the car with Ward and they went away together into the night."

"That was when you first stopped?"

"No, sir. It was during the second stop."

"Do you mean when the car was already turned around to go back toward Tucson?"

"Yes, sir. I never saw her again."

"Corporal Van Fleet."

The corporal was clearly at the end of his tether. His nerves, for one reason or another, were jumping. Any slight shock would have pushed him over the edge so that he would lose control. His face was anguished and his fingers were constantly working; he did not know where to direct his glance.

"You heard the question, Corporal?"

O'Rourke leaned over the prosecuting attorney, who then said, "Let me underline the fact that you are speaking under oath and let me remind you that perjury is a Federal crime which lays you open to a penalty that might amount to as much as ten years in prison."

Van Fleet was as painful to look at as a wounded cat on whom overexcited urchins continue to vent their rage. For the first time, the full drama was in evidence. At this precise moment, the baby who belonged to the Negro mother began to cry. The coroner, impatient, scowled. The mother tried in vain to quiet the child. Twice, at the exact moment Van Fleet opened his mouth to speak, the baby cried even louder, so that finally the young Negress decided regretfully to take the child out of the courtroom.

Then Pinky opened his mouth once more and his mouth stayed open without a single sound coming out of it. The silence seemed so long that it compared well with Pozzi's two or three minutes on the highway. Everyone wanted to help the corporal, almost to cue him to give an answer, as if they were ready to ask the coroner not to browbeat the young man any further. Once more O'Rourke leaned over the prosecuting attorney; the latter got up, walked straight over to the witness bench, and behaved in the manner of a schoolmaster.

"You heard Pozzi's deposition? When you stopped by the side of the road, your friend Wo Lee was the only one waiting there. Where were you?"

"In the desert."

"On the side near the tracks?"

"Yes."

"On the tracks?"

Van Fleet shook his head frantically, no.

"No, sir. I swear that I never put my feet on those tracks."

"But, from where you stood, couldn't you see the tracks?"

No answer. He looked all around the room and yet at no one. Maigret had the impression that he was making an enormous effort not to turn his gaze on O'Neil.

Drops of sweat were visible on his forehead, and once more he began biting his nails.

"What did you see on those tracks?"

The young man did not answer, struck dumb with panic.

"In that case, please answer the first question. When did you last see Bessie, dead or alive?"

The agony on the young Dutchman's face was such that several people's nerves began to tingle and a few almost wished to cry out "Enough!"

"I said, dead or alive. Did you hear me? Please answer."

Then Van Fleet jumped up and burst into sobs, shaking his head violently.

"It wasn't me! It wasn't me! . . ." he cried, gasping. "I swear it! It wasn't me! . . ."

He was trembling from head to foot in an agony of nerves, his teeth rattling and his gaze wandering in a frantic manner from one to another around the room. He could not have focused on anyone.

O'Rourke quickly drew close to him and grabbed an arm firmly. He had to hold him very tight. Otherwise, the young man would have thrown himself to the floor. He led him toward the door and put him into the hands of big Gerald Conley, the deputy sheriff with the revolver that had a carved handle.

Then he spoke to Conley in a low voice and went to talk, afterwards, with the coroner.

One felt the indecision, the floating atmosphere, of the room. The prosecuting attorney went to the coroner in his turn, and they conferred together for a few moments. Then all of them seemed to be looking for someone. From the corridors Hans Schmider was retrieved, the man who had discussed the footprint and who once more had a package in his hand.

Turning toward the Negro on the jury, the coroner murmured: "If you'll permit us, we are going to listen to this witness before putting your question to the two remaining men. Please come here, Schmider. Tell us what you discovered during the past night."

"I went to the base accompanied by two men and we searched the refuse that was waiting to be burned. This is gathered in an open area a little distance from the actual barracks. We had to use flashlights. Well, to make it short, this is what we found."

From a box he pulled out a pair of low shoes, far from new, and, showing the undersole, pointed to the rubber heels.

"I compared these with the footprints. These certainly are the shoes that left the traces of number two."

"Please explain."

"I called traces of number one those that fell approximately from the car that was by the road to the railroad tracks. These more or less followed the footprints made by Bessie Mitchell. Traces number two are those that begin farther along the road in the direction of Nogales and end up at the same point on the tracks, not far from the spot where the body was found."

"Were you able to decide to whom these shoes belong?"

"No, sir."

"Did you ask people at the base?"

"No, sir. There are about four thousand men."

"Thank you."

Before he left, Schmider put the shoes on the prosecuting attorney's table.

"Corporal Wo Lee."

When he was called, the Chinese returned to the witness stand and once more they had to lower the microphone for him.

"Don't forget that you will be giving your testimony under oath. I am going to ask you the same question I asked your pals. When did you see Bessie Mitchell for the last time?"

He began without hesitation. Yet he paused as he habitually did, with the look of one who is mentally translating the question into his own language.

"When she got out of the car for the second time."

"And you didn't see her again after that?"

"No, sir."

"And you didn't *hear* her either?" the attorney, with whom O'Rourke had been talking in a low tone, interrupted.

This time the young Chinese took longer to think it over. He looked at the floor for a moment, opened his large eyes wide, and said, "I am not sure, sir."

Immediately he looked for O'Neil, his eyes pleading, as if he were asking forgiveness.

"Exactly what do you mean?"

"I heard some noises as if people were quarreling, and then I heard a rustle of bushes."

"At what point was this?"

"Perhaps ten minutes before the car drew up."

"You mean Pozzi's car?"

"Yes, sir."

"You were on the road?"

"I never left it."

"Had the taxi been sent back long before?"

"Perhaps a half hour earlier."

"Where had your pals gone?"

"When we left the taxi, first we all walked together in the direction of Nogales, as I told you. I think we had missed the spot and we'd stopped a little too near the airstrip. After a little while, we turned halfway around and separated. I continued to walk along the road. I heard Van Fleet about twenty yards into the desert, and O'Neil was even farther away."

"Was he as far away as the railway tracks?"

"Just about. At a second point, I heard noises."

"Did you recognize a woman's voice?"

"I'm not sure."

"Did that go on for a long time?"

"No, sir. It was very short."

"You didn't hear the voice of either Van Fleet or O'Neil?"

"I think I did."

"Which of the two?"

"That of O'Neil."

"What was he saying?"

"It sounded confused. I think he was calling Van Fleet."

"Did he call him by name?"

"No, sir. He called him Pinky, as he usually did. Then someone started to run. I had the impression that people were talking in low tones. That's when I saw a car coming toward us from Nogales and I moved out into the road to get him to stop."

"Did you know your two friends would come and join you?"

"I thought that when they heard a car stopping they would come."

"Any questions, Mr. Prosecutor?"

He shook his head.

"What about you, gentlemen of the jury?"

They, too, said no.

"Court adjourned!"

9

The Sergeant's
Hip Flask

Maigret tried in vain to stop O'Rourke as he sped by. Busy as he was, he had passed quickly and closed himself in his office on the ground floor. The window was open because of the heat, and Maigret could see an endless passing of people back and forth during the adjournment.

Pinky was there, seated on a chair near the green file cabinets. He had been given a drink to settle his nerves. O'Rourke and one of his men spoke gently to him, as if to a friend, and two or three times the corporal seemed to give a weak smile.

The Negress walked back and forth in the corridors constantly, with her baby in her arms and her brothers and sisters making a sort of escort. When the jurors were called to resume their places, she was the first to take hers in the seats for the public.

Definitely, everything was conducted more or less as it would have been in France, with the single difference that in France the questioning would have taken place in the offices of the Judiciary Police, behind closed doors, instead of taking place in public.

The jurors seemed somehow more sober, as if they felt the hour of their responsibility creeping up on them.

Without the Negro's question, would the inquiry have taken the same turn? Would O'Rourke, then, have taken charge of the whole operation?

"Sergeant Van Fleet!"

He now looked like a boxer who had been clobbered during the previous rounds and who rises once more to face his adversary, awaiting the knock-out blow, so that one watched him with a certain degree of compassion.

Everyone knew that he knew, and everyone wanted to know the truth at last. At the same time, they were a little ashamed that they had been forced to reduce him to such a state. The coroner left the job of finishing him off to the prosecuting attorney, who got up once more and went toward the witness, his portfolio in his hand.

"About ten minutes before the car arrived that brought the three of you back to the base, something happened on the railroad tracks, the sounds of which had been heard from the road. Did you hear them?"

"Yes, sir."

"Did you see anything?"

"Yes, sir."

"Exactly what happened?"

It was clear that he had made up his mind to tell everything. He looked for the right words to blurt it out. For a while, it seemed as if he would have to turn to someone for help.

"Well, it had been quite a while now that Ted had been going to bed with Bessie. . . ."

It was strange to hear him call O'Neil at this moment by his first name.

"I suppose I must have made a noise without wanting to."

162

"How far were you from the couple?"

"Five or six yards."

"O'Neil—did he know that you were there?"

"Yes."

"Had you arranged this between you?"

"Yes."

"Who bought the hip flask of whiskey? At what point was it bought?"

"It was a little before the closing of the Penguin Bar."

"At the same time as the other bottles?"

"No."

"Who had the idea?"

"The two of us."

"You mean to say O'Neil and you?"

"Yes, sir."

"What was the intention behind your buying a bottle which you could slip in your pocket when you had been drinking all evening and you were going to drink more when you got to the musician's house?"

"We wanted to get Bessie drunk, and Sergeant Ward never let her drink as much as she wanted to."

"At the musician's you already knew exactly what you wanted to do?"

"Well, perhaps not exactly."

"Did you know that you were going to wind up the night in Nogales?"

"There or anywhere else, it would all happen more or less the same way."

"To sum up, before you left the Penguin Bar, that is, before one in the morning, you both already knew what you wanted?"

"We said that perhaps we would have a chance to work it out."

"Was Bessie in on the plan?"

"She knew that Ted had gone several times to the Penguin Bar to meet her there."

"Was Wo Lee in on the secret?"

"No, sir."

"Who had the bottle in his pocket?"

"O'Neil."

"Who paid for it?"

"The both of us. I gave him two one-dollar bills. He added the rest."

"But there was already another bottle in the car."

"We weren't sure that they would leave it there. Besides, it was a big fat bottle that we couldn't have hidden."

"When you left for Nogales and O'Neil found himself in the back seat with Bessie, did he try to take advantage of the situation?"

"I suppose so."

"Did he give her a drink?"

"Possibly he did. I didn't ask him."

"If I understand you, it suited you two just fine when Bessie was left out in the desert."

"Yes, sir."

"Did you discuss it between you?"

"We didn't need to talk about it because we understood each other."

"Did you decide at that point that you wanted to get rid of Wo Lee?"

"Yes, sir."

"You had not foreseen that Ward and Mullins would return to the desert?"

"No, sir."

"Did you expect that Bessie would consent?"

"She had already had a lot to drink."

"And you expected to give her more to drink, right?"

"Yes, sir."

At this point, the witness would have answered the most embarrassing questions.

"How is it that it took you almost a half hour to find Bessie Mitchell?"

"We had stopped the taxi too short. Also, we'd been drinking. It's hard at night to make out the road in the dark."

"You tried once more to send Wo Lee back, didn't you? When you had both gone into the desert?"

"Yes, sir."

"Were you together?"

"Yes. O'Neil was on my right, maybe twenty yards away. I could hear his footsteps. From time to time, he whistled softly to let me know where he was."

"So he found Bessie on the railroad tracks?"

"No, sir. Right nearby."

"Was she sleeping?"

"I don't know. I think so."

"Then exactly what happened?"

"I heard him speak to her softly and I figured that he was stretching out near her. She thought, first of all, it was Sergeant Ward. Then she burst out laughing."

"Did he give her something to drink?"

"He must have, because I heard the noise the empty bottle made when it was thrown on the pebbles, probably in the direction of the track."

"What were you doing meanwhile?"

"I was coming closer, as quietly as I could."

"Did O'Neil know it?"

"He must have known it."

"Was this the understanding you had between you?"

"More or less."

"That's when something unexpected happened, isn't it?"

"Yes, sir. I must have hung up on a bush and made a

noise. Then Bessie started to swing at him and got furious. She yelled that she understood everything, that we were a dirty bunch, that we took her for a whore, but that we were wrong. O'Neil tried to calm her down, afraid Corporal Wo Lee would hear her."

"Did you keep going nearer?"

"No, sir. I wasn't moving at all. But she could see my silhouette. She kept on yelling at us, telling us what bastards we were and promising that she would tell Ward all about it. She said he would break our jaws for us."

He was speaking in a monotonous voice amid absolute silence.

"Did O'Neil have his arm around her?"

"She told him to let her go and she was fighting with him. Finally she got free and started to run."

"On the tracks?"

"Yes, sir. O'Neil ran after her. She could scarcely hold herself upright and zigzagged from one side to the other. She stumbled several times on the ties. Finally she fell."

"Then what happened?"

"O'Neil hollered, 'Are you there, Pinky?'"

"I went toward him and heard him grumble, 'What a bitch!'

"He asked me to go after her to see if she had hurt herself. I told him that he should go since I didn't feel I had the nerve to do it. At this point, I felt really sick. Then I heard a car on the main road coming to a stop. I heard Wo Lee calling us."

"So nobody went to see what condition she was in at this point?"

"Finally O'Neil went. He just leaned over. He held her hand but he didn't really touch her."

"What did he say when he came back toward you?"

"He said, 'She played a dirty trick on us. She isn't moving.' "

"Did you decide that she was dead?"

"I don't know. I couldn't ask any more questions. The car was waiting for us. We could see the headlights. We could hear the driver's voice."

"Didn't you think about the train?"

"No, sir."

"Didn't O'Neil mention it?"

"We didn't say a word between us."

"What about back at the base?"

"No. We went to bed without saying a word."

"Any questions, gentlemen of the jury?"

They did not move.

"Sergeant O'Neil."

The two men crossed paths near the witness box without looking at each other.

"When did you see Bessie Mitchell for the last time?"

"When she fell on the tracks."

"Did you lean over her?"

"Yes, sir."

"Had she hurt herself?"

"I thought I saw a little blood near her temple."

"Did you decide that she was dead?"

"I don't know, sir."

"Didn't the idea occur to you to take her somewhere else—at least to move her?"

"I didn't have time, sir. The car was waiting."

"Didn't you think of the train?"

There was a second's hesitation.

"Not in any precise way."

"When you found her near the tracks, was she asleep?"

"Yes, sir. She woke up almost immediately."

"Then what did you do?"

"I gave her something to drink."

"Did you have sex with her?"

"Well, I began, sir."

"What interrupted you?"

"She heard some noise. When she saw Corporal Van Fleet's silhouette, she understood, and she fought against me, calling me all sorts of names. I was afraid Wo Lee would hear us. I tried to make her shut up."

"Did you strike her?"

"I don't think so. She was drunk. She scratched me and I tried to make her listen to reason."

"You had every intention of killing her to make her shut up?"

"No, sir. She got away from me, and she began to run."

"Do you recognize these shoes? Do they belong to you?"

"Yes, sir. The next morning I thought that they might find the footprints in the sand, so I threw them out."

"Any questions?"

When O'Neil had left the witness box, the coroner called, "Mr. O'Rourke."

The latter simply got up without leaving his place.

"I have nothing to add," he said, "unless anyone has any questions to ask me."

He looked modest, almost astonished, as if he had had no part in what had just taken place, and Maigret grumbled between his teeth, "You old fraud, you!"

Then, like a man worn out by toil, the coroner read the text to Ezekiel giving the charge to the jury. Ezekiel replied in kind, swearing that he would protect the jury members from any possibility of entering into communication with anyone whatsoever during the period of the jury's deliberations.

The coroner followed this up with a few explanations to the five men and one woman. The audience saw them disappear into another room, whose stout oak door then closed behind them.

On the balcony, the same white shirts were to be seen, cigars and cigarettes reappeared, as, of course, did bottles of Coca-Cola.

"I think you have plenty of time to go have lunch," said O'Rourke to Maigret. "Either I'm very much mistaken or they'll take at least an hour or two."

"Did you read my note?"

"Forgive me, it completely slipped my mind."

He took the envelope out of his pocket, opened it, and read a single word, "O'Neil."

Just for an instant, his slightly smug smile left his face while he observed his colleague. "Had you understood, too, that he hadn't done it on purpose?"

Instead of answering, Maigret questioned him in turn:

"What kind of sentence will he draw?"

"I'm wondering if I could accuse him of rape, since at the beginning of the month the girl had already consented. Also, he didn't strike any blows that we know of. The only thing against him in any case is false testimony."

"Then that should draw about ten years?"

"That's just about it. They're nothing but kids, dirty kids all right, but kids, aren't they?"

Probably both of them were thinking of Pinky and his crisis of conscience. The "kids" were not very far away, all five of them. Sergeants Ward and Mullins looked at each other hard-eyed, as if they were mutually suspicious.

Were they going to get together, become friends as they had been before? Would they just wipe away past history as if off a slate?

Ward, after some hesitation, accepted the cigarette that Mullins offered him, but he didn't say a word for the rest of the session.

Wo Lee had done what he could to answer honestly all the questions that had been put to him, without in any way accusing one of his comrades. All alone, he stood against a column drinking the Coca-Cola that someone had been kind enough to bring him.

Van Fleet was talking in a low voice with the deputy sheriff, Conley, as if he still felt some need to justify his own extreme reactions; meanwhile, O'Neil, also alone, his face hermetically sealed, furiously stared at the patio in which the spurts of water tried to freshen the patches of brown grass.

"Dirty kids!" O'Rourke had said, now ready to plunge into a new inquiry.

As if he could find a way of reestablishing relations, he suggested to Maigret:

"Let's hoist a quick one, shall we?"

Was there any reason why they should not reestablish the cordial relations and the sense of good-humored companionship they had enjoyed the day before?

They went together toward the corner bar and found several of those with whom Maigret had spent the previous two days as a member of the audience. Nobody wanted to discuss the case. Each was drinking his glass by himself.

The sun played among the multicolored bottles on the shelves. Someone had slipped a coin into the slot of the jukebox. An electric fan whirred slowly over the bar, and, outside, automobiles passed, sleek and shiny.

"Sometimes it happens," Maigret began in a hesitant voice, "that one feels cramped in a ready-made suit that is cut too close at the seams. Sometimes the discomfort becomes actually intolerable and one longs to tear the whole thing off."

He slugged his drink down in a single draft and asked for a second. He remembered the various confidential bits and pieces Harry Cole had passed him, evocations of thousands of men—hundreds of thousands of men—all of them in bars, who, all at the same time, were drowning their consciences in the same nostalgia, expressing the same impossible need, and who, on the following morning, with the help of a cold shower and a powder from the famous blue bottle, would become good fellows once more, men without ghosts.

"There is no doubt about it, accidents do happen," O'Rourke sighed, carefully cutting the point of a cigar.

If Bessie had not heard any noise . . . If in her drunken state she had not imagined that she was being treated as a whore . . .

Five men and a woman—oldsters, a Negro, an Indian with a wooden leg—were gathered together under Ezekiel's surveillance and were trying to arrive at a just verdict in the name of conscientious, organized society.

"I've been looking for you for the past half hour, Julius. How long will it take you to pack your bags?"

"I don't know. Why?"

"My colleague in Los Angeles is eager to see you. One of the best-known gangsters in the West was shot down a few hours ago, just as he was coming out of a nightclub in Hollywood. My pal is convinced this would interest you. We can catch a direct plane out of here in an hour."

Maigret never saw Cole again, nor O'Rourke, nor the five men from the Air Force. He never knew the exact verdict. He didn't have even the time to buy the postcards showing the cactus flowering in the desert, which he had promised to send his wife.

In the plane, he wrote on a pad of paper propped on his knees:

My dear Madame Maigret,

I am having an excellent trip, and my colleagues are extremely kind to me. I think basically the Americans are kind to most everybody. As for my describing the countryside for you, that's a hard task; just guess that I have spent ten days without even wearing a jacket! And I am sporting a cowboy belt around my waist. Still happy that I haven't been "had," because I would now be wearing cowboy boots and a broad-brimmed hat such as they wear in the Far West films!

In fact, I have reached the Far West and at this moment I am flying over the mountains where one still finds Indians with feathers on their heads.

What seems to me unreal is our apartment on Boulevard Richard-Lenoir and the little café on the corner which serves me my Calvados.

In less than an hour, I will land in the world of the cinema stars and then . . .

When he woke up, the pad of paper had slipped from his knees. A stewardess as pretty as a magazine cover girl gently adjusted his seat belt across his ample stomach.

"Los Angeles coming up!" she told him.

He perceived that they were heading down fast and

that the plane was already banking. There below lay a vast stretch of white houses set amid green hills just by the side of the sea.

Whatever would he see now?

July 1949